The Color of Tenderness

The Color of Tenderness
(A cor da ternura)

JABUTI PRIZE WINNER, 1990

Geni Guimarães
ILLUSTRATED BY **SARITAH BARBOZA**

TRANSLATED AND INTRODUCED BY
NIYI AFOLABI

AFRICA WORLD PRESS
TRENTON | LONDON | CAPE TOWN | NAIROBI | ADDIS ABABA | ASMARA | IBADAN | NEW DELHI

AFRICA WORLD PRESS
541 West Ingham Avenue | Suite B
Trenton, New Jersey 08638

Copyright © 2013 Geni Guimarães
Translation: © 2013 Niyi Afolabi
First Printing 2013

All rights reserved. No part of this publication may be reproduced, stored in a retrieval system or transmitted in any form or by any means electronic, mechanical, photocopying, recording or otherwise without the prior written permission of the publisher.

Book and cover design: Saverance Publishing Services

Library of Congress Cataloging-in-Publication Data

Guimarães, Geni.
  [Cor da ternura. English]
  The color of tenderness / Geni Guimarães ; translated and introduced by Niyi Afolabi.
     pages cm
  A translation from Brazilian Portuguese of A cor da ternura.
  Includes bibliographical references.
  ISBN 978-1-59221-924-7 (hard cover : alk. paper) -- ISBN 978-1-59221-925-4 (pbk. : alk. paper) 1. Guimarães, Geni--Childhood and youth. 2. Guimarães, Geni--Family. 3. Women authors, Brazilian--Biography. 4. Women, Black--Brazil--Biography. 5. Blacks--Brazil--Ethnic identity. 6. Brazil--Social conditions. I. Afolabi, Niyi. II. Title.
  PQ9698.17.U363Z46 2013
  869.1'42--dc23
                              2012050811

To my friends,
Johannes and Moema Parente Augel,
Who, with their unique affectionate warmth,
Saved me so forthrightly from the timidity
Of my own internal world

CONTENTS

Introduction
Magic of Words: Gender, History, and Afro-Memory
Niyi Afolabi
- ix -

Color of Tenderness

- -1-   First Memories
- -17- Lonesome Voices
- -23- Affinities: Eyes Within
- -33- Journeys
- -41- School Days
- -51- Metamorphosis
- -63- Foundation
- -69- Becoming a Woman
- -75- Crystal Moment
- -79- Fluctuating Energy

Magic of Words: Gender, History, and Afro-Memory

Niyi Afolabi

Preamble: *Color of Tenderness*

At a time when race relations continue to divide more than provide a road map to genuine equality among different people across cultures, nations, and religious beliefs, Geni Guimarães's *A cor da ternura* (1989) continues to be relevant, over twenty years after its publication. The issues of invisibility and marginality do have their place and one may add that as this is an autobiographical piece, Guimarães may not have set out to be ideological *per se*, since most of the instances of racial tension portrayed in her novella are subtle, anecdotal, reconciliatory rather than indicting. This may be predicated on the original target audience—seemingly juvenile, yet the material is serious enough to appeal to a broad readership, confirmed by the prized Jabuti award. When the overall *oeuvre* of Geni Guimarães is placed in the context of Afro-Brazilian struggle, the recent works by Dawn Duke (*Literary Passion*), Emanuelle Oliveira (*Writing Identity*) and Niyi Afolabi (*Afro-Brazilians*) confirm that she has made cogent contributions in the area of "Gender, History, and Afro-memory" that constitute the focus of this commentary on her semi-autobiography.

What are the concerns of Geni Guimarães in *A cor da ternura*? Her characters, mostly within the family circle, and others within the school and neighborhood setting, interact with such a sense of distance that tension is implied in their relationships. For someone writing and publishing in the 1980s, it is lamentable that she could not be more direct in her descriptions of moments of racial tension among her characters. Instead, symbols and sarcasm become strategies of indictment, opposed to aggressive confrontation. This can be seen as a matter of style, but the autobiography presented by Geni Guimarães glosses over the issues of disenfranchisement, poverty, inequality, and deprivation. The reader is left to question why a specific situation is as it is but the writer does not articulate a direct disavowal of racial inequality even through the omniscient narrator's perspective. This distancing strategy may have the effect of presenting the reader with the history of Brazilian intergenerational dynamics and how race relations have affected every area of society, black Brazilians most negatively.

With a very delicate sense of purpose, Guimarães exposes us to her childhood memories without judging the participants. Instead, she presents moments as factual and innocent—often even playful—from the viewpoint of a child. The narrative voice is that of a child; this perhaps accounts for narrator's lack of commentary about the political and racial climate of Brazil. Perhaps only from this perspective can we appreciate this narrative as a piece of autobiography written from the viewpoint of an innocent child. Structured in ten chapters that capture the evolution of this observant young woman from her infancy to her adolescence, we follow the story and her attachment to her mother, father, other siblings, and surrounding figures—ranging from extended family and "grandmother" figures, to curious establishment figures and classmates.

From the viewpoint of gender relations, it is curious and pertinent to note that the narrator focuses more on female figures than on males. For example, while the reader learns of Guimarães's father through descriptions of family celebrations, we are told little about the father later in the narrative. Instead, emphasis is placed on female characters such as her mother, her older sisters, and the grandmother figures, suggesting a subconscious feminine world as prioritized by the narrator. The title in this sense may be relevant: the "color of tenderness" could refer to an ambivalent manifestation of tension emanating from the color of one's skin as well as the supportive family setting that provides balancing tenderness. This unspoken tension between racial discrimination and family support problematizes the apparent simplicity and accessibility of the text, inviting the reader to examine issues that are more subtly raised. Oftentimes, the party who discriminates against another feels better in terms of saving the face when the issue is presented as not deliberate but caused by ignorance and need for better understanding of human relations.

The childhood world of Geni Guimarães is a rural family circle composed primarily of women. Her older sisters, Cecília, Arminda, and Iraci took on the responsibility of protecting Geni and explaining life to her since her mother was pregnant with her younger brother soon after her birth. Likewise, her adolescent world was enhanced by the presence of "grandmother" figures, such as Chica Espanhola and Vó Rosária. While these maternal figures are not directly living within Geni's household, they are indirectly present in her life. Chica Espanhola was noted for her ability to provide traditional healing for the little girl on several occasions, and Vó Rosária functioned as the family matriarch although she lived in a different house. She was known and loved for her storytelling prowess and all the children looked forward to her stories, which served as a way of passing down social values and morals to the younger generation.

The Color of Tenderness has given us an invaluable window into the world of Geni Guimarães while making a statement on racial discrimination in Brazilian society at the same time. In questioning issues of absence, marginality, invisibility, racial violence, ignorance, racial inequalities, and prejudices, tempered with the stoicism and determination to tell her story of triumph, the author has not only intimated us with Afro-Brazilian culture, she has endeavored to challenge the vestiges of racial discrimination through her mastery of language that she calls the "magic of words." What other testament could match the closure of the narrative in which Geni Guimarães synthesizes her intentionality and the burden she carries as a writer and an Afro-Brazilian woman: "Prone to my messianic mission and style, I am a pastor of my people; fulfilling with pleasure the right and responsibility to take them to harmonious places. My coat of arms I have since discovered and kept always ready; above, below, and in the middle of the magic of words."

The narrative itself would be incomplete, without the creative and imaginative illustrations of Saritah Barboza. The panels further heighten the finesse of the work by providing visual interpretations of verbal imprints. As the translator of this work, I am humbled by Guimarães's ingenuity and sensitivity.

Intertext of Gender, Nation, and Identity: Geni Guimarães's Literary *Corpus*

Of the entire generation of cultural producers who belong directly or indirectly to the *Quilombhoje*[1] move-

---

1. This a literary and political organization located in São Paulo, Brazil, that emerged in 1978 through the production of an annual literary production, *Cadernos Negros*. Although it did not officially become known as *Quilombhoje* until 1980, most of the members share the same ideology about the recuperation of African values and dignity for Afro-Brazilians in general. For an in-depth study on the movement, see Chapter 2 of *Afro-Brazilians: Cultural Production in a Racial Democracy* (New York: University of Rochester Press, 2009), 51-79.

ment, Geni Guimarães[2] is one of the most mature and by far, the most accomplished, with awards ranging from the coveted Jabuti Prize in 1988, the Adolfo Aisen prize in 1989, to the Black Personality award in 1990. She writes poetry as well as fiction, and also writes children's literature. The body of her work reveals a playful writer who on the one hand combats racism and sexism, and on the other, unaggressively situates the Afro-Brazilian experience within the totality of Brazilian reality. Yet despite her record of productivity, the critical reception of her works is scanty, a situation that is not limited to Guimarães alone.

The criticism of Afro-Brazilian literature is generally faced with a dilemma Cuti (Luis Silva) qualifies as "intellectual orphanage"[3] which may be extended to critical orphanage. The lack of a systematic body of critical works[4] geared toward the recognition of valuable works and their authors makes the critical inquiry of an "outsider"

---

2. Geni Guimarães's extensive literary corpus includes, *Terceiro filho* [Third Child] (poems) (1979), *Leite do peito* [Chestly Milk] (children's short stories) [1986], *A cor da ternura* [Color of Tenderness] (novella) [1988], *Balé das emoções* [Ballet of Emotions] (1994), *A dona das folhas* [Goddess of Leaves] (Childrens' literature) [1998], *O rádio de Gabriel* [Gabriel's Radio] (Children's literature) [1998], *Aquilo que a mãe não quer* [That Which Mother Doesn't Want] (Children's literature) [1998]. Others are scattered in various anthologies in Europe, the United States, and Brazil.
3. See Cuti, "Fundo de Quintal nas Umbigadas," *Criação Crioula, Nu Elefante Branco* (São Paulo: Secretary of Culture, 1986, 151-160). By "orfandade intelectual," Cuti is referring to the ignorance of most Afro-Brazilians about their own literary past as well as a certain shame and disdain by those who do know. He cites some examples of important writers of the past: Cruz e Souza, Lima Barreto, Machado de Assis, and Luiz Gama—all of whom have been accused, myopically of course, of one form of "betrayal" or the other. According to Cuti, contemporary critics need to know Afro-Brazilian intellectual history to do justice to the critical opinion on recent works.
4. Other than works by Zilá Bernd, Luiza Lobo, and a few unpublished dissertations on Afro-Brazilian cultural production, *Quilombhoje* only boasts of two collective critical works which are lacking in depth but do serve as useful introduction to the works of the group, namely *Cadernos Negros*, but not to the works of individual writers.

particularly daunting. Even among the "insiders" such as the authors themselves, criticism is an elitist endeavor and not many can afford the luxury. The result is a plethora of panoramic reviews in local magazines, especially during a book's launch. The challenge for the individual and group producer such as *Quilombhoje* is how to move the accomplishments of the movement to the academic setting, which continues to marginalize their relevance. It is arguable, in fact, that individual Afro-Brazilian writers such as Miriam Alves, Geni Guimarães, Esmeralda Ribeiro, and Cuti, are better known and recognized for their works outside of Brazil than within Brazil.

Born September 8, 1947, Guimarães belongs to the generation I have designated as "forerunners of Afro-Modernity"[5] in the sense that they matured at a time of political openness in Brazil—a period which led to the formation of many cultural and political entities such as the *Movimento Negro Unificado* (Brazilian Black Movement), *Ilê-Aiyê*, *Olodum*, and *Quilombhoje*, among many others. She qualifies as the "total" Afro-Brazilian writer in the sense that she does not confine herself to labels of race and gender although her writings do manifest passionate sensibilities concerning the plights of Afro-Brazilian women, men, and children. In a response to a question about her function as writer in the Brazilian society, she asserts, in a recent interview:

> Acredito que o escritor, compromissado com seu povo e sua época, deve cumprir o dever de conscientizar, denunciar e reescrever a história de forma a provocar transformações sociais que impulsionem o indivíduo em busca de uma sociedade melhor e mais humana.[6]

---

5. See Chapter 9, "The Forerunners of Afro-Modernity," *Afro-Brazilians: Cultural Production in a Racial Democracy* (New York: Rochester University Press, 2009), 207-238.
6. Interview with Geni Guimarães in Barra Bonita, São Paulo, Brazil—July, 2001.

> I believe that a writer, committed to her people and her time, must fulfill the duty of raising consciousness, contesting and rewriting history in such a manner that provokes social changes which spur the individual into searching for a better and more humane society.

This global perspective is essential as the Brazilian woman writer must not function in an esoteric feminist vacuum, but in the reality of home, work, society, culture, and racism. Celeste Dolores Mann captures the multiple function and responsibilities of the Black woman writer in general when she posits that in addition to dealing with white male domination, the Brazilian woman writer must engage in a "constant process of debunking myths, deconstructing cultural paradigms, attacking stereotypes and defining their own voice [...]. Moreover, much of the writing is a search for racial, cultural, or female identity. Because of the dominant society's concept of racial identity, its myth of racial democracy, sexism, and paternalism, this quest is extremely complex for Afro-Brazilian women."[7] It is within this "complexity" that the literary corpus and significance of Geni Guimaraes must be understood.

Woman as the "Continual Motion" of the World

In assessing the creative world of Geni Guimarães, Conceição Evaristo's poem, "Eu—Mulher" [I—Woman], provides several "epigraphic" insights that capture the ancestral linkage as well as the feminine strength of this

---

7. See Celeste Dolores Mann, "The Search for Identity in Afro-Brazilian Women's Writing: A Literary History," *Moving Beyond Boundaries (Vol. 2)*, Carole Boyce Davies ed. (New York: New York University Press, 1995.), 173-174.

multivalent writer—attributes that both define, pervade, and illuminate the imagination in *Terceiro Filho* [Third Child], *A Cor da Ternura* [Color of Tenderness], *Balé das Emoções* [Ballet of Emotions], and *Leite do Peito* [Milk from the Heart]:

> Uma gote de leite / me escorre entre os seios. / Uma mancha de sangue / me enfeita entre as pernas / (...) / Eu—mulher em rios vermelhos / inaugura a vida. / (...) Antevejo / Antecipo / Antes-vivo. (...) / Eu—Mulher / abrigo da semente / moto-contínuo / do mundo.[8]
>
> [A drop of milk / runs down between my breasts. / A stain of blood / adorns me between my legs. / (...) I foresee / I anticipate / I live beforehand. (...) / I—Woman / shelter of the seed / continual motion / of the world].

The representation of the woman as life-giver, as the repository of strength, and as the "vital engine" that propels the world, connects with the power of the ancestors to provide solace in times of weakness, vision in times of blurriness, and assurance in times of uncertainties, to the extent that the woman may be seen as protector of the "seed" of life, just like the ancestors. Women and the ancestors are connected not only physically but spiritually, hence the analogy captured in the qualities of "foresight," "anticipation," and "life-before and life-after." A new child born has a lineage that transcends the immediate parents but continues his or her linkage with the great parents and the ancestors. In African cosmological belief, these ancestors are not dead and gone but are still co-mingling with the living, manifesting themselves through animate and non-animate objects.

---

8. See Conceição Evaristo, "Eu—Mulher," *Enfim...Nós / Finally .. Us*, Miriam Alves and Carolyn Richardson Durham, eds. (Colorado Springs, Co: Three Continents Press, 1995), 71. The English translation cited is by Carolyn Durham.

Guimarães's poetic corpus, from *Terceiro Filho* through *Balé das Emoções* as well as her anthologized[9] poems, shares the qualities of Conceição Evaristo's epigraphic poem. In the "continual motion" metaphor are embedded issues of love, life, death, the anguishes of racism and sexism, as well as efforts to make the world a better place. The entire collection seems to be guided by a synesthetic sensibility between bondage and freedom, between a gendered tension and a penchant for compassionate humanity as illustrated in the poem, "Livre" (Free) which may be regarded as her "arte poética." The poet comes to terms with the limits of the poetic word to capture the "heart of the poet," the "infinite sadness" of the world, the "happiness of the universe," and concludes rebelliously that "all the goodness of the soul cannot be boxed into one sonnet." Guimarães's philosophy of poetry is evocative of what Harold Bloom calls "the anxiety of influence"[10] or rather the internal tension suffered by the poet in the process of freeing himself or herself from other external "inevitable" influences in the poetic process. In "Livre," Guimarães asserts her rights and the imperative to be free:

> Por isso é que agora me liberto / E liberto a profusão de alegrias que há em mim / E liberto a liberdade de minha liberdade, / E solto o mundo reprimido. / (...) / Na liberdade de meu verso eu vibro, / Eu amo, eu canto! / Eu me completo e completo o meu poema. /

---

9. See for example, Paulo Colina ed., *Axé: Antologia Contemporanea da Poesia Negra Brasileira* (1982); Oswaldo Camargo ed., *A Razão da Chama: Antologia de poetas negros brasileiros* (1986); Oswaldo Camargo ed., *O Negro Escrito* (1987); Moema Parente Augel ed.,*Schwarze Poesie - Poesia Negra* (1988); and Miriam Alves & Carolyn R. Durham eds. *Enfim...Nós / Finally Us* (1995).
10. In *The Anxiety of Influence*, Harold Bloom suggests that in the process of negating the influence of the previous generation, a given poet ends up affirming that generation even if the product of that negation seems to be new and different.

> Eu sou gente, eu sou mulher, criança. / Livre!!! (*Terceiro Filho* 56).
>
> [That is why I set myself free / I set free the torrent of happiness within me / And I set free the freedom of my freedom / And I release the repressed world. / (...) / In the liberty of my poetry, I vibrate, / I love, I sing! / I complete myself and complete my poem. / I am people, I am a woman, I am a child. / Free!!!].

There is nothing else to add to this explicit poetic vision: Guimarães revels in her freedom within the inescapable bondage and conditionings of the world. In the Brazilian racial context where the potential for veiled discrimination is rampant, the freedom to self-express directly or indirectly is a powerful consolation that cannot be taken for granted.

Of the entire poetic collection in *Terceiro Filho*, only a few poems address issues of blackness directly or indirectly. Instead, Guimarães focuses more on the frustrations of love, the freedom to express herself, the acceptance of death as an inevitable "nothingness" in life, and varied philosophic reflections that depict her wisdom and compassion for humanity. The freedom of expression that Guimarães holds so dearly in "Livre" (Free) is contradicted in another poem, "Contradição" (Contradiction") where the poetic voice admits that faced with the immensity of the space in the universe, freedom becomes frightening especially as she ponders the sensation that a poet is more often living "in prison" that living in freedom in the sense that the poet is constantly running away from herself: "Andei sob medidas, / Com medo de me encontrar. / (...) / Mas tanto tempo estive presa, / Que meteu-me medo a liberdade, / E fiquei completamente accorrentada, / Com todo este espaço que existe no universo. (86) [I walked in calculated precision, / With the fear of finding myself. / But for a long time I was stuck, / That freedom gave me the fright, / And I was completely overwhelmed, / With all this space in the world]. An explanation for this contradiction may be found in "Banalidades" (Banalities), the closing poem, where the poet imagines what her legacy would be, expecting the reader to conclude: "para cada louco, uma mania..." (119) [For every insane mind, a mania...]. On the contrary, Guimarães is not an insane poet, rather she may be translating the traumatizing potential of the world's harsh realities.

Beyond the contradictory freedom in "Contradição," only in "Palco da vida do crioulo" [Life Stages of the Bi-Racial] does Guimarães critique the positive but romantic image of the bi-racial or crioulo as the miscegenated figure or "native-born slave" who is supposed to be representative of the cosmic race that Brazilian race-mixture policy has created. Instead, Guimarães inverts and subverts that image by portraying the anonymous bi-racial as orphaned, poor, uneducated, miserable, homeless, and alcoholic. Here is an ideological poem—subtle yet effective as it ridicules the Brazilian myth of racial democracy. In the last stage of the bi-racial life, he dies of misery and hunger in the company of his friend and killer—cachaça: "Um crioulo embriagado. / E onde estava ele, lá se via ela: / Na rua, no quarto, no bar, na calçada, / Na fome, na sede, na dor, na miséria, / Morte-mulher em gota disfarçada, / Ma companhia, namorada sincera" (13-14). [A drunk native. / And where he was, there she was: / In the streets, in the room, in the bar, on the stairway, / In hunger, in thirst, in pain, in misery, / Mother-Death in veiled drops, / Bad company, honest girlfriend]. "Palco da vida do crioulo" is ironically a simultaneous critique of Brazilian typical rum (Cachaça) in view of its destructive potential on its victim.

Guimarães's concern for the downtrodden and the marginalized is also echoed in "Você é responsável" (You are responsible) where she shares her elation ("sentir-me árvore" [feeling like a tree]) at being pregnant with others, and upon the birth of the child, provides advice to all children about their role in shaping their own destinies: "Não vi no meu filho um marginalizado, / Um jovem ladrão, vadio, assassino. / Não me vi dando ao mundo um filho viciado!" (10) [I could not see my child as a marginal, / a young rogue, a loafer, an assassin. / I could not see myself giving birth to a corrupted child!] Similarly, Guimarães critiques laziness and ignorance as represented in "Tereza Molecada" [Frivolous Tereza] who spends her entire life having babies, one after the other, without any education, exposure, discretion or wisdom. The poetic voice not only condemns the marginal-assassin child, she also ridicules the irresponsible mother with a sarcastic series of questions: " Oi Tereza, como vai a vida? / Já sarou a barriga do Matéus? / E ela, responde boca escancarada: / "Tá tudo bom, com as graças de Deus" (89). [Hello, Tereza, how is life? / Has your stomach recovered from having Mateus? / And she replies, mouth wide opened: / "All is well, by the grace of God"]. The "Frivolous Tereza" figure goes against the notion of the woman as a "continual motion" of the world in the sense that instead of engineering the world wisely, Tereza has become a danger to that process since her children will not have adequate nurturing or provision but will end up as the assassins and rogues that Guimarães protests in "Você é responsável." A final message to the youth is captured in "Droga... Que Droga, Bicho?" [Damn... Damn, Dude?] where the poet advises young ones to be involved in their own future and not live a futile life: "Voce simplesmente não está. Vocé néo é homem! / (...) / Faça uso da sua mocidade. / Não seja apenas uma desculpa na terra. / Você pode nascer amanhã, / E ser um presente para a sociedade (36). [You are simply not present. You are not a man! (...) / Cultivate your youth / Do not be a sorry statistic on earth. / You can be born tomorrow, / And be a present to the society]. Although these social concerns relating to the youth and single mothers indicate a social consciousness on the part of Guimarães, her overall political consciousness is questionable.

Terceiro Filho resonates in other socio-emotional and philosophical spheres in which Guimarães's "politics" seems blurred. As most of her "reflective" poems aptly indicate ("reflexão" [15, 76, 88]), the poet seems to be content with the status quo or to accept social conditions she sees herself as unable to change. The only solution she proposes is to "make the best of life" as in "Reflexão": "Se ... / Deus existe com sua misericórdia e com sua justiça, Não me preocupo com o que há de vir, / Porque ... / Neste mundo em que vivi, / Do modo em que as coisas são. / Eu vivo do modo que me é possível" (76). [If... / There is merciful and just God, / I do not worry about tomorrow, / Because ... / In this world that I live, / The way things are. / I live by the rule of possibility]. While the temptation to shrug off overwhelming social injustices as the inscrutable will of God is certainly understandable, it is also arguable that to be socially inactive is escapist. Religion can only provide some succor, but the harsh realities which make life unlivable for many people are experienced on a daily basis, and are rectified through political and social change. Whether or not Guimarães's indifference is a survival strategy created for a very hostile environment, it speaks to her "conservatism" as captured in "Indiferença" (Indifference). Her expression of a total disenchantment with life and her willingness to accept whatever life has to offer suggests a lethargic spirit conditioned by the shock of racism and limitations that she does not address directly in a collection she has interestingly titled "third child." "Indiferença" captures Guimarães's lethargy very vividly: "Se eu tiver que ser feliz, que seja! / Se tiver que sofrer, que sofra! / Onde quer que eu esteja, / Apenas faço questão desta indiferença (114)." [If I have to be happy, so be it! / If I have to suffer, so be it! / Wherever I am, / I only insist on this indifference].

A cursory look at the remaining poems reveal a tormented life challenged by a permanent search for love and the realization of non-fulfillment as in "Mãos Vazias" [Empty Hands], where Guimarães is filled with pessimism and emptiness since she is constantly giving and not receiving in return. The question the poet seems to be asking is: How can I console others when I am tired and empty with nothing else to offer? The image of the "empty hands" symbolizes both the giver and the receiver. This total self-resignation is captured in the last stanza: "Canso-me é certo, mas não paro nunca, / Encarreguei-me de viver assim. / Então, eu tenho que dar sempre o que não tenho, / Resigno-me e vou: Exausta, pobre, indiferente. / De braços abertos e mãos vazias (78). [I am tired of course, but I stop never, / I chose to live like this. / Hence, I have to give what I don't have, / In self-resignation, I continue: Exhausted, poor, indifferent. / With open arms and empty hands]. Similar somber poems, such as "Constatação" [Realization], "Pensei" [I thought], "Meu Grande Pequeno Mundo" [My Great Little World], "Morte" [Death], "Crise" [Crisis], "Final de Buscas" [End of Searches], and "Consequência"—all depict the poetic voice contemplating and dealing with pain and suffering, death and its acceptance, as well as disillusionment, as if the poet were preparing the reader for the inevitable in this world: peaceful death. Yet, the poet's worldview is the pleasure of making others happy despite the persistent obstacles as in "Meu Mundo" [My World].

What is saddening in this poetic trajectory lies in the poet's self-analysis in "Canstatação"—a feeling that the aggressive experiences of life and nature have schooled her to the extent of becoming a thorn, a stone, a disgrace — negative attributes that reflect a stoic and indifferent posture in the face of the adversity of life. As the poetic voice asserts: "Concluí a auto-avaliação: Longe dos rios me tornei o lodo, / Fugindo das rosas me tornei o espinho. /

Sou pedra sem montanha. / Sou bagagem dos caminhos em que andei (16). [I concluded the self-analysis: Far from the rivers I became the mud, / Running from flowers I became a thorn. / I am the stone without a mountain. / I am the street baggage on the paths I walked]. It takes a strong woman to be a "continual motion" in spite of the obstacles the world seems to put on the way of the poet. The motions and emotions in *Terceiro Filho* call attention to the ancestral strength that Afro-Brazilian women may not even be aware of but evoke through resilience and hope embedded in their works.

Much of these feelings of frustration and betrayal are resultant from unreciprocated love that pervades *Terceiro Filho*. At least half of the entire collection evokes emotions of love--be it desire, passion, longing for a lost lover. Guimarães, in this sense, is a lover who never grows old. In fact, she offers a theory of being a woman in "Para Ser Mulher" [To be a Woman]. According to her, a woman needs to play many roles at the same time: she is wife, lover, and mother while seeing beauty as a desirable complement to those qualities, not an essence or requirement. In addition to having "girlish" looks, she must be womanly in her decisions, "dizer sim e sem dizer não, saber negar" (108) [saying yes, and without saying no, knowing how to refuse]. She must also be able to articulate a "maybe" with her head and have a "theorem" in her body—but in any instance must she be ignorant. A series of poems relates the pain and suffering of the poetic voice such as "Dúvida" [Doubt], Falando de Amor [Speaking of Love], "Orgulho" [Pride], "Dor Sublime" [Sublime Pain], "O que Amo em Você" [What I love about You], "O que Digo e o que Dizem" [What I say and What They Say], "Meus Dias Felizes" [My Happy Days], "Meu Fadário" [My Destiny], "Alegria de Ser" [Joy of Being], "Comunhão" [Communion]. As painful as most of these "love" poems are, they nonetheless provide

xxiii

solidarity for all women as they share in the hardships and pleasures of loving in a patriarchal setting such as Brazil.

Terceiro Filho may be considered a book of love presented to women in particular and to humanity as a whole. "Dúvida" expresses a sense of loss of a loved one and the love-hate memories that follow being jilted. "Falando de Amor" is a definition of love by a passionate lover. "Orgulho" captures the ego of a lover which gets in the way of true expression of love but instead manifests itself as pretense and pretexts. "Dor Sublime" expresses the suffering of love during a conflict or unexpected disappointment. "O que eu amo em você" declares love in spite of the other's negation and indifference. "O que digo e o que dizem" evokes a poet in love and the suffering generated by love—the poet hides her feelings but her soul declares a deeper love. "Meus Dias Felizes" captures the sad nostalgia of the woman as she discovers an old love letter. "Alegria de Ser" contends that being in love gives the poet a fascinating sensation of beauty, affection, and satisfaction. "Comunhão" describes sexual act as a process of irrationality and insanity and yet, a desirable moment of exchange between two people in love or in lust: "E fica sempre, / Tapando-me a boca, / Cegando-me a visão, / Para que eu possa fingir o meu riso, / E no meio dos meus gestos, / Nos instantes de protestos, / Não mostrar que a desrazão de te querer, / Deixou-me louca (104). [And stay for ever, / Tapping me in the mouth, / Blinding my vision, / In order for me to fake my smile, / And in the midst of my gestures, / During instants of protest, / Not to show the irrationality of wanting you, / Made me crazy].

Despite the agony of love that encompasses most of the poems in *Terceiro Filho*, the poetic voice seems to be on a permanent search for the ideal love, especially in the poem she calls "Meu Fadário" [My Destiny]. Partly pessimistic, and partly optimistic, "Meu Fadário" is a poem of hope for love. Four movements can be identified in the structural world of the poem. In the first movement, the poetic voice—poor, spiritually dead, and unloved—longs to know her destiny. In the second movement, a startling and hopeful destiny is revealed: an ardent passion and a sublime lover. In the third movement, the passionate love is lost, grief follows, the poet feels like dying. Finally, in the fourth movement, hope comes alive as a prediction is made: "um dia virá quem tanto quero" [One day, the one I want so much will come]. It is on this positive note that "Meu Fadário" projects a brighter future for the tired and disillusioned lover. The "continuous motion" in *Terceiro Filho* is an explosive adventure domesticated through the power and subtlety of poetic language. Although not declared as an "autobiography," it contains insights into the life and times of the poet—if the poetic voice is taken (hypothetically) as the individuality of the poet herself. It is no surprise then when in "Consequência," Guimarães alludes to Cecília Meireles's poetry when she states: "Sou poeta. / Não sou alegre nem triste. Caí na indiferença, / Quando vi e ouvi a condição de existir nesta vida (44). [I am a poet. / I am neither happy nor sad. / I slid into indifference, / When I saw and heard the living condition of this world]. This conclusion is similar to that reached by Cecília Meireles when in "Motivo" (Motive) she self-defines: Eu canto porque o instante existe / e a minha vida está completa. / Não sou alegre nem sou triste. / Sou poeta. [I sing because the moment exists, / and my life is complete. / I am neither happy nor sad. / I am a poet]. The blatant identification with Meireles partly explains the abstraction in Guimarães's poetry. Meireles lost her parents very early in life while Guimarães lost many lovers and loved ones. Both dealt with their disillusionment through sensuous enchantment with nature and total liberty of the spirit found in poetry.

Unlike *Terceiro Filho* which was dedicated to the poet's father, *Da flor o afeto, da pedra o protesto* [From

Flower an Affection, From Stone a Protest], a second volume of poetry, is dedicated to Guimarães's mother, and sister Cema—an interesting division of affection between parents and a sibling. The title offers some clues: "flower" represents affection while "stone" represents protest as if to suggest a poetic evolution or even paradigmatic shift from ideological conservatism[11] to consciousness and confrontation. While *Terceiro Filho* "explodes" with inequalities in love and a sense of disenchantment with the world, *Da flor o afeto* takes a more pragmatic position in indicting racial oppression and discrimination. For a poetry that has been conservative so far, it is refreshing to have at least three poems which deal with Brazilian racism. "Integridade" [Integrity], "Negrinha" [Young Black Woman], and "Explicação" [Explanation] may either be appreciated separately or analyzed as a triad. They contribute to the intertext of gender, nation, and cultural identity that defines some of the concerns of Afro-Brazilian women writers. The first makes a declaratory statement where the poet defines herself as a proud Afro-Brazilian woman. The second calls to awareness and action by young black women and by extension, herself. The third poem explains her newly found consciousness to all who may be confused by this sudden change in poetic strategy and language. Both the

---

11. When compared to Esmeralda Ribeiro, Sônia Fátima Conceição, Miriam Alves, and Coceição Evaristo, Geni Guimarães seems less forceful in articulating racial issues, at least in *Terceiro Filho*. Perhaps this explains why, to date, there is no study of a "racial" nature regarding Geni Guimarães while others have enjoyed comparative studies especially with more established Brazilian women writers such as Carolina Maria Jesus and Clarice Lispector. Some have even enjoyed comparative studies with Afro-American writers such as Alice Walker, Maya Angelou, and Toni Morrison although most of these studies are still yet to be published. In most cases, they are on-going doctoral dissertations in Comparative Literature or essays-in-progress. See for example Lesley Feracho, "Transgressive Acts: Race, Gender and Class in the Poetry of Carolina Maria de Jesus and Miriam Alves" *Afro-Hispanic Review* 18.1 (1999): 38-45.

title and the cover have prepared the reader: a young boy stands with an aggressive posture, as if protesting or attacking an adversary. Since Guimarães has insisted on poetic liberty, this analysis does not concern itself with what led to this change—for other poems in the volume also address issues of love, gerontology, and loneliness—but they are overall less abstract and more pragmatic. As a "continuous motion" that moves the world, the reader is rolling along with the motions and emotions of Guimarães's poetic progression.

"Integridade," as the title suggests, is the totality of an individual when assumed and defended. It is a cogent statement on identity—individual, collective, and cultural. "Integridade" enumerates what it takes to be considered an "Afro-Brazilian woman" without shame. The pride of being a "black Brazilian woman" runs through the poem and even more compelling in the last stanza, where the poetic voice sounds even very "purist" as she emphatically affirms: "Negra / Puro Afro sangue negro, / Saindo dos jorros, / Por todos os poros" (8). [Black Woman / Pure Afro black blood, / Gushing out, / Passing through all the pores]. This call to assume one's identity, one's heritage, one's history, and one's past is a Pan-African sentiment since the poetic refers to black blood in general. The qualities of blackness are enumerated in the crispy hair, shining back, rhythmic walk, black hands, black breasts, black soul, black sensibility, black truths and lies, black cries and smiles and finally, black blood. The poem's title can be replaced with "identity" for ultimately, that is what black integrity is all about. The first line of each stanza repeats "ser negra" (being a black woman) for rhythmic emphasis and musicality while finally breaking to the word "Negra" (Black Woman), as if referring to all black women.

In "Negrinha," the poetic voice dialogues with a young black woman she sees in a hanging portrait. In the portrait, this young woman is sitting in the lap of a Santa

Claus, almost in a kneeling posture and looking in only one direction. The poet observes the youngster as sad in her smiles, with short curly hair and a closed mouth. Her entire demeanor angers the poet to the point of hurt and revolt that she critiques the little girl's silence and voicelessness: "Em pé negrinha! / Levanta os bracos, / Estica as pernas! / Escancara a boca! / Diz que tem fome, / Grita que tem sede!" (9). [Get up, young black woman! / Raise your arms, / Move your legs! / Lively up your mouth! / Say that you are hungry, / Cry that you are thirsty!"]. The context is ironical in the sense that Santa Claus is usually a loving and caring figure who provides for the needy but in this case, the girl is expected to ask for help and gifts. Likewise, what the girl needs is more than a gift: In fact, she is hungry, depressed, and voiceless. The awareness that the poetic voice is providing the girl is only an incentive, a call to action and to protest. It is only at the end of her poetic action that she realizes that she was speaking to a portrait and not the girl herself: "Perdão: / Quase me esqueço que a negrinha, / Só é um quadro pendurado na parede..." (9) [Sorry: / I almost forget that the young black woman, / Is only a portrait hanging on the wall...]. The poem is one more example of a shifting ideological consciousness of Geni Guimarães which locates her within the intertext of gender, nation, and cultural identity.

After these well articulated poems about blackness, beauty and sensibility, Guimarães feels the need to explain her ideological position—an uncomfortable plight that reinforces the tensions of racial relations in Brazil. Without mentioning the word "racism" in "Explicação" [Explanation], Guimarães craftily indicts the myth of racial democracy, pointing out its hypocrisy and its debilitating effects on Afro-Brazilians. At the very beginning of the poem, the poetic voice declares: "Não sou racista" (13) [I am not racist]. This assertion seems to be a defensive answer to a question or rumor concerning her ideology; that she has responded at all is curious. On the one hand, every artist has the right to express himself or herself and to choose his or her subject matter freely. Yet, censorship is normal in dictatorial Brazil which only started changing in the mid 70s. On the other hand, the burden to have to explain oneself on such an issue is a double jeopardy. The usual excuse for critics of those who raise their voices against racism or any form of discrimination is to label those entities as "racist" or "segregationist" so as to put them on the defensive. If defending one's culture and identity is "racist," perhaps it is best for it to be thus. Responding artistically in her second work is a creative response that is commendable in this sense. After admitting that she may be considered "doida" (crazy), she confesses that she is only human and that she cries like everyone else and this poem is not seeking revenge for social inequalities. Rather, she simply wants to "Banir dos nossos peitos, / Este sentir hereditário e triste, / Que muito me magoa / E que tanto te envergonha." (13) [Banish from our hearts, / This hereditary and sad feeling, / Which hurts me / And which shames you so much]. It is instructive to note that instead of using the words "racism" or "superiority complex," she uses terms such as "hereditary," "sad," "shameful," and "hurtful." I do not consider Guimarães's choice as "poetic" license *per se* but a conscious and convenient effort not to offend anyone, especially since she already feels compelled to "explain" her ideological position. The use of the affective pronoun "te" also betrays this familiarity, as if talking to a friend. Of course, the means is effective in the Brazilian context and the mission completed but the attitude of the poetic voice is (un)consciously condescending. Guimarães's *Da Flor o Afeto* announces a poet whose "motto" indeed is to be "free" to express herself as she pleases without constraints.

With *Balé das Emoções* [Ballet of Emotions], Guimarães returns, once again, to a "sanitized" poetry where words are suggestive and racial or social-political issues must be read between the lines. The volume opens with an epigraph by Paulo Bonfim which suggests, ironically, that we write in such a manner that posterity will be able to decipher effortlessly, "a cor do nosso sangue" (10) [the color of our blood]. Perhaps this is an unconscious betrayal of guilt or a caveat for the reader who may raise questions after reading—for in actual fact, there is no art to finding the color of blood—it is red. "Blood" in this context seems to mean origin, race, species, or temperament. As the title suggests, the collection is a "ballet of emotions" in terms of a theatrical dancing performance characterized by movements and fluidity—indicating a lack of formal constraints and rules.

Published in 1994, fifteen years after her first book of poetry, *Balé das Emoções* fails to capture the intensity of the previous collections in the sense that the concerns of the poetic voice have become quite banal and popular. An allusion to Adélia Prado's "Com Licença Poética" gave some expectations especially with regards to the creative process as a "parto sem dor" (36) [a painless delivery], but upon a closer analysis, poetry is manipulated as a "warning finger" – in the sense of a coded expression that has the potential to liberate or to indict . A few of the poems are noteworthy, such as "Condição" [Condition], in which the poetic voice invites a lover to recognize her appeal as an "aroma of Africa" (66). In "Lembranças" [Memories] the poet remembers and pays homage to older and contemporary intellectual artists such as Camões, Drummond, Meireles, Cuti, Oswaldo, Colina, Semog, and Graciliano (84); "Magia Negra" [Black Magic] describes the value of unity and invisibility in love: "Somos um e ninguém vê. / Nem nós" (98) [We are one and no one notices. / Not even us]; and "Visão de Mim" [Vision of Myself] offers a reflection on the poet's life and achievements—and the incompleteness she feels at death's figurative approach. One of the most compelling poems in *Balé das Emoções* is

"Queda do Pássaro" [Fall of the Bird], a tragic narrative of the life of a bird, from its struggle with the currents of life, and without much struggle, falls into a heap of grass. In empathy, the poetic voice identifies with the bird, claiming personal knowledge of the bird's fate: "Comungo-me com ele / pois sei de sua sorte: Morre da dor singular de ser sozinho" (80). [I commune with it / for I know about its fate: It dies of a singular pain of loneliness]. In her mid-fifties, Guimarães seems concerned about her final years but she is not as frail as her contemplative poems suggest. Perhaps her evocation of death and acceptance of its inevitability is a direct inspiration from the ancestors with whom she is very much in communion.

While Guimarães may be cryptic and subtle in her poetry, she is more revealing in her prose, as demonstrated by her autobiographical mementos in both *Leite do Peito* and *A Cor da Ternura*—narratives about rites of passage from infant black girl through adolescence in Brazil's "racial paradise." Since *A Cor da Ternura*, [Color of Tenderness] a novella published in 1988, is a reworked version of *Leite do Peito* [Milk from the Heart] (*a collection of short stories* published two years earlier), I focus this analysis on *Leite do Peito* as an "expanded" version of *A Cor da Ternura*. Both titles reflect the maternal and sensitive instincts of the young Guimarães as she recounts memories of her growing up black and female in a racist society. As the *Jornal Nacional do Movimento Negro Unificado* reports: "Espanta-me como a autora consegue colocar, purificar e cristalizar em formas literárias tão belas, momentos tão amargos da sua/nossa experiência com o racismo brasileiro"[12] [I am terrified how the author is able to translate, purify, and crystallize through such beautiful literary forms, such bitter moments of her/our experience with Brazilian racism].

---

12. Editorial review quoted in *Jornal do Movimento do Negro Unificado* 6 (1989) [Salvador-Bahia-Brazil] during the launching of *Leite do Peito*.

In eleven short stories, and from "Primeiras lembranças" [First Memories] through "força flutuante" [Fluctuating Energy], Guimarães portrays the ugly faces of discrimination and the virtue in breaking racial barriers through loving oneself and others. Guimarães recognizes that her memories have not come from "nothingness" but from her parents, siblings, and children to whom she pays homage for their contribution to her "tenderness and transparent soul" (11-12). In a recent interview with Guimarães, the writer states: "Although many walls have been torn down all over the world but for Afro-Brazilians especially, other walls still need to be broken since they are cleverly disguised. We can only achieve this through unity of the race and it is not enough to keep saying 'yes, sir' to everything and everyone but we need to take our struggle to the political arena."[13] In real life, Guimarães is more down to earth; as a writer, she carries her artistry to the formal level—recounting memories with such great creative imagination that she seems both detached and deeply attached to the events in her narrative. The artistic distance does not limit her vision of infancy, femininity, blackness, and a curious questioning of the world of adults. In addition, Guimarães exposes other perplexing images, such as her thoughts on Christmas as a commercialized event, the irony of the omniscience of God, the violence perpetrated against black Brazilians through the myth of racial democracy, evocation of respect for the elderly and their wisdom, and a subtle critique of the educational system and the educators. Such a broad scope of concerns is definitely not that of a child and *Leito do Peito* is a voice of a young Guimarães captured by the adult.

"Primeiras Lembranças" [First Memories] is a tapestry of domestic and urban events crystalized into one short story. Young Guimarães finds herself in a caring and

---

13. Interview with Geni Guimarães in Barra Bonita-São Paulo-Brazil, July, 2001.

loving family where her close attachment to her mother is fundamental as echoed in their mother-child conversations, their playfulness in action and in words, her own realization of her challenged sister, Cema, whom she calls "exceptional, my stupid poet" (19) and her curiosities about childbirth and where babies come from –especially when her mother becomes pregnant. In this story, the qualities of tenderness are laid out as captured in the title, *Leite do Peito* itself, and in the novella it later produced, *A Cor da Ternura*. Tenderness is captured in the mother's witty patience in explaining and answering all questions raised by the young Guimarães; it is captured in the milk the young child reaches for in her mother's chest, it is captured in mother's answer in a child's moment of doubt about love:

> — Mãe, a senhora gosta de mim?
> — Ué, claro que gosto, filha.
> — Que tamanho? - perguntava eu.
> Ela, então, soltava minha cabeça, estendia os braços e respondia, sorrindo:
> — Assim. (15)
>
> — Mother, do you love me?
> — Don't be naughty! Of course, I do, my daughter.
> — About what size? — I asked.
> She will then stretch her arms over my hair and answered with a smile:
> — This big.

Despite young Guimarães's innocence, she is also able to empathize with her sister, Cema, by cleaning her with her own clothes when Cema, due to her mental challenge, eats dirt. In the poem dedicated to Cema in *Da Flor o Afeto*, "Cema, Ceminha," adult Guimarães would later share the wisdom of this "exceptional" sister: "Mentira do mundo que a Cema é bobinha. / A Cema é poeta" (2) [A lie of the world that Cema is stupid. / Cema is a poet]. Even when Guimarães is in doubt, she asks her sister about the existence of God for example. Cema replies by pointing to objects around the house to suggest that God is everywhere and in everything.

While "Primeiras Lembranças" sets up the family setting, a microcosmic Afro-Brazilian social reality, "Bairro da Cruz" [Da Cruz Neighborhood] expands on that setting to an entire neighborhood. Since Guimarães's mother is a school teacher, the family contemplated moving from the rural area to the city. The decision to move involved everyone in the family meeting to discuss it. This democratic decision-making is contrasted against the description of a typical Sunday afternoon, which is typically a day of leisure for men who spend it playing soccer. Women, on the other hand, have their labor pre-determined and divided: some clean house, some prepare lunch, others do the laundry and shine the shoes. Guimarães is charged with taking care of her siblings: her mentally challenged sister, Cema, and the youngest, Zézinho.

The discussion of the move is illuminative—it reveals the concerns of everyone as well as the support to move to a new neighborhood and house. As usual, it is mother of the house who raises concerns:

> — O Bairro da Cruz e estranho, sei la. Tem um povo ma-encarado, esquisito. O vizinho da comadre, mesmo, ja teve preso. Parece que se apossou de coisa alheia. Tenho medo que as criancas peguem maus costumes. Deus me livre! - disse minha mae, se benzendo. (94)

> [—The Da Cruz neighborhood is strange, who knows. You have a strange kind of folks there. Even a neighbor of our godmother got arrested. Seemed like he had possession of a controlled substance. I am afraid the children will pick up bad habits. Lord have mercy! -- my mom stated, blessing herself].

This episode exemplifies the migration patterns even within a state—from the more rural to the more urbanized setting. In addition, it mirrors the democratic setting of the Afro-Brazilian family against the stereotypically macho and autocratic living usually portrayed by biased writers.

"Education," whether formal or informal, cannot be divorced from rites of passage. "Tempos Escolares" [School Days] exposes the internalized violence and double standards caused by racial discrimination in Brazil. Discussions about Princesa Isabel, the historical princess figure who signed the abolition of slavery into law, made interesting instruction for the youngsters who listened attentively to the stories told by grandmother Rosária—a white version of the slavery where slaves were represented as "simple," "passive," and religious. By inserting this important episode in the history of Brazil, especially about slavery, Guimarães succeeds in retelling the history to all who may want to forget its significance and ambivalence especially in Brazil. The irony of the story lies in the fact that, despite this allusion to abolition of slavery, the reality is that "slavery" was still being practiced through racial discrimination. On at least two occasions, young Guimarães had a conversation with her mother about dress codes and hygiene. Her mother wanted her to be clean and well kept but she wonders why Janete could be untidy and she could not. Her mother's response says it all: "—Mas a Janete é branca" (45) [—But Janet is white]—suggesting that Janet could get away with what young Geni Gumarães could not. This "inferiority" complex becomes internalized as a code of conduct—as the young student unconsciously reminds herself every day: "Nariz limpo. / Eu era negra...a Janete, branca... / -- agora e na hora da nossa morte..." (49) [Clean nose. / I was a black girl...Janet, white ... / -- now and even till death...]. Guimarães's painful realization of discrimination seems tragic and traumatic for the little black girl to the extent that reminding herself becomes the only way to cope with a social injustice she feels condemned to and which she cannot change—at least, that is the impression her mother gives her so that she get accustomed to the normalized absurdity.

After the initial lessons on "racial democracy" in "Tempos Escolares," other episodes crystallize the transition of Guimarães from a girl to a woman, especially "Metamórfose" [Metamorphosis] in *Leite do Peito*, and "Mulher" in *A Cor da Ternura*. These two interrelated stories provide the decisive moments in the formation of Guimarães as a woman. In addition to being an intellectual guide for generations born and yet unborn, and as the "continual motion" of the world, a woman undergoes physical and hormonal changes to prepare her for reproduction, motherhood, and nurturing. "Metamórfose" continues where "Tempos Escolares" ends in terms of additional details on the significance of Princesa Isabel. The young narrator quickly discovers a disparity between Grandmother Rosário's version and that of her teacher: "Hoje, comemoramos a libertaçao dos escravos. Escravos eram negros que vinham da África. Aqui eram forçados a trabalhar e, pelos serviços prestados, nada recebiam. Eram amarrados nos troncos e espancados, às vezes, até a morte" (62) [Today, we commemorate the freedom of slaves. Slaves were blacks who came from Africa. Here, they were forced to work and for their labor, they received nothing. They were tied to poles and beaten, at times until death]. The conflicting versions don't stop her from internalizing racial inferiority as she questions her own talent and courage to produce and read her poetry. She experiences mental agitation and insecurity when she thinks there aren't any black heroes or ancestors from whom to draw inspiration and strength. To the contrary, there are black heroes and heroines such as Zumbi dos Palmares and Luiza Mahin, but these were not taught at the time. The

Magic of Words: Gender, History, and Afro-Memory

narrator loses confidence in herself to the extent that she not only was able to present her poetry on Princesa Isabel but tried to "wash off" her own blackness using material used to clean dirty aluminum pots. She hurts herself badly enough to cause bleeding, but relizes she cannot change her color. This episode confirms the conclusions of psychologists on the potential damage of discrimination to blacks in general.

For a woman, the experience of life is incomplete without the ritual that confirms her femininity. Guimarães's day comes when she begins to menstruate and quickly seeks her mother's help for the blood which at the time was incomprehensible to her:

> Fiquei apavorada. Que seria aquilo, meu Deus? Por que saia tanto sangue de dentro de mim, sem mais nem menos? (...)
> — Mãe, olha... Acho que arrebentou tudo quanto e veia. Me ajuda! (...)
> — Você virou mulher, besta. Prá todo mundo e assim. Eu, a Arminda, a Iraci, a Maria, a Cecília, até a Cema passamos por isso. E assim mesmo que acontece. (*A Cor da Ternura* 79)
> [I became terrified. What could that be, my God? Why is so much blood gushing out from within me, no more no less? (...)
> — Mother, look ... I think that all my veins have been ruptured. Help me! (...)
> — You just became a woman, stupid. For everyone it is the same. For me, Arminda, Iraci, Maria, Cecilia and even Cema, we went through the same thing. That is how it happens].

From this moment on, Guimarães is growing up to be a woman with the challenges and opportunities that accompany this transformation. Above all, she also realizes that discrimination does not end with graduation. Even as a teacher, she was observed more often than others and a few white students expressed concerns about having a

xxxvii

black teacher: "Eu tenho medo de professora preta" (87) [I am afraid of a black teacher]. The fear, of course, comes from the negative and stereotypical instruction that this particular white young girl has received from the society—principally her white family. Guimarães's *Leite do Peito* as well as *A Cor da Ternura* both capture the ingenuity of a writer who struggles to achieve symphony and harmony in a racially discordant "paradise" such as Brazil.

A mature and award-winning writer, Guimarães has taken Afro-Brazilian (women's) writing to a visible and respectable level through a consistent outreach to the wider Brazilian society and her socio-artistic efforts to bring all races and ages together. Along the line of these efforts, she has focused her attention on children's writing as a way of reaching the children before society reaches them. At least three of her children's books have been published and adopted in schools in addition to *A Cor da Ternura*—which appeals to both adults and children. Others include *A Dona das Folhas* (1993), *O Rádio de Gabriel* (1993), and *Aquilo Que a Mãe Nao Quer* (1998). These works are ample indication that Geni Guimarães is the classic representation of what Conceição Evaristo calls the "continual motion " of the world—especially her determination to create awareness in the hearts of those who still perpetuate racism—or claim that it does not exist. The challenge to appreciating her literary corpus lies in translating her seven texts to date as well as her numerous collaborations with other writers in anthologies of which only a handful are currently available in English.

The Color of Tenderness
(A cor da ternura)

First Memories

My mother would sit in a chair and remove her smock while I would reach out to her. She would place me within her thighs and tuck her hands inside the lower neck of her dress from which she removed her breasts and gave me her milk while standing.

She would seize the occasion to remove lice from my hair or comb my hair. At times, we struck a conversation:

- Mother, do you love me?
- My goodness! (Ué!) Of course I do, my daughter.
- How much? I asked.

She would then release my head, extend her arms and respond with a smile:

- This much.

I would return to her breasts, with eyes closed, and suck happily.

That was the extent of the sure love I needed. I could not imagine any other kind of love beyond the extension of her arms.

On other occasions, in the midst of sucking, I would stop to ask:

- What happened to my bacon?
- The cat ate it.
- Where is the cat?
- Went to hunt the rat.

- Where is the rat?
- Went to the bush.
- Where is the bush?
- Fire burnt it.
- Where is the fire?
- Water quenched it.

I would interrupt the playful questions to further ask her things well beyond her own imagination. Once, it went like this:

- Who made fire and water?
- Of course, God. Who else could it be?
- And if fire should break out in the world?
- God would turn water into rain and quench the world's fire.
- Mother, should there be divine rain, will it be my kind of color?
- Goodness! There is nothing like colored rain. In case there is any such thing, if at all possible, you know what would happen? She picked me up, tickling me in the belly, and said: - You would become white and I remain black, you white and I black...

Suddenly, we stopped laughing and playing. A strange silence ensued between us.

I thought she was sad, hence I spoke:

- Stupid lie. My skin color will remain the same still. You think I would leave you alone? Not me. Never, never, never; not a chance, ok?

Then she pretended to be spanking me mildly while she took off running for the verandah outside.

- Whoever arrives last will become a lagoon's toad.

I ran as well, taking long steps, trying to keep up with her track.

But things started to change. I only had to ask for her breast milk and she would avoid me.

- Cecília, she would call, bring my daughter's squash.

On other occasions, I only needed to hang on to the tip of her dress; she would quickly come up with alternatives: a home-made candy, a guava, an orange or anything with glucose to keep me at bay.

One day, I got very upset. I threw away everything she gave me. I refused to eat anything. Then she decided to explain her situation to me:

- Your mom's milk is now rotten.
- Who made it so? I asked innocently.
- Maria Polaca's cat defecated on my breasts.
- Why did you let him get in there, mother?

She did not reply. She called Cecília and said:

- Take her to see the pigs. Then quietly: - Don't let her see the pigs milking because she may get "ideas."

We left and I was weeping quietly while wiping my face with my back hands. Suddenly, a stripped cat ran in front of us and I remembered something.

- Cecília, on which part is the entrance to mother's head?

My sister looked both ways; she saw a stone in the middle of the road. She sat on it and explained to me affectionately:

- Look, let me explain this to you clearly. Mother ordered another baby for us. You are now much older, you have grown teeth, you can now eat everything you want, can't you? But the baby cannot. As a result, mom has to save her milk for the baby. Understand?
- Oh, that was why mother went to the city the other day... Cecília, how is the .... going to be? How is the baby going to look?
- He is going to be a fat, beautiful, crybaby. She replied with a smile.

I lowered my head and started digging holes in the sand. Cecília got up, put me on her neck and started walking off. I started feeling sleepy and asked:

- If he comes in the evening, you let me know...

Feeling relaxed around her neck, I dozed off.

She was beautiful. I would never forget to look at her. All day long, she dragged her slippers all around the house. She went up and down.

I also went up and down with her. Whenever she picked me up flagrantly, imitating her gestures, I would smile calmly and briefly. My heart was almost jumping out with joy within me.

I would lower my head and close my eyes. I relived her smile a thousand times and in the evening, I would

First Memories

sleep much sooner in order to think of her sweet aroma of mother and land.

One day, when I was inspecting her legs, I found out that they were swollen. I started observing more closely: the thighs were unusually big. Her belly looked like the pot in which she kept the drinking water: Hands, arms, face, everything was swollen. I started trembling and became impatient. What kind of sickness could that be? What if my mother was getting ready to explode?

I became desperate.

I needed someone to explain to me if she was getting ready to die. I needed to know if she was dying, if we could all die as well. I ran out to the yard. Then I saw Cema, my older sister. I ran towards her. I shook her up terribly. I asked, cried, insisted, but Cema kept eating a cob and sifting out the leftover shell through the sides of her mouth. In my desperation, I had forgotten that she was unique, my stupid poem.

With my blue flowered outfit, I cleaned her mouth, held her hands, and waited patiently for someone to arrive. Before long, I saw Arminda coming from the corner. She had gone to take lunch to my father and other brothers who were working at the coffee factory. I released Cema's hands and went to meet her.

- Arminda, I said, I think our mother is going to die. Please, take her to Madam Chica for final rites and blessings. She is like this big. I extended my arms on both sides and made a circular sign to indicate the size of her belly. - Arminda, I continued, please take her.

She lifted me up gently and affectionately and started to caress me.

She responded:

- Your mother is not sick, silly. Remember that Cecília told you that mother had ordered a baby? You already know, then. She is being kept in her belly; that is why your mother's belly is so big. Aren't you sleeping with me? Of course, so as not to hurt the baby.

I murmured:

- Arminda, I love you, but I would like to sleep with mother, because her ears are quite soft and they warm up my hands. You are also a nice person but your ears ...

I cried again, calmly and quietly. When I arrived at home, my mother was sewing a quilt-type shirt while standing, leaning on the turned off stove. Arminda appeared suddenly and told her:

- Someone needs an outfit. Give it to me so I have just finished patching.

My mother gave the outfit to Arminda and sat in a patched chair. She spread her arms and I felt like being transported to the heavens. I became all furious and could not hold my head on her always friendly breasts. In the meantime, I did not say anything. I did not thank her. I did not complain. I simply breathed in profoundly to recover the eternal aroma of mother and land.

One day, upon waking up, I did not hear any noise, nor feel the pleasant aroma of the freshly brewed coffee coming from the kitchen. I was all alone in the bed. I was all set to find out what was going on when Iraci entered the room saying:

– You need to stay here quietly. You cannot get up yet.

I noticed her affectionate gesture but I was worried. I asked a thousand questions, all at the same time:

– Why not? Where is Arminda? Where is mother?

I was sobbing, swallowing my tears of fright and uncertainties when Iraci precipitated herself and explained:

– Arminda went to work and I am substituting for her. Don't you worry. Father went to pick up Madam Chica Espanhola. Mother is sleeping.
– Madam Chica Espanhola? I asked, all worried.
– Don't be silly, nothing is the matter. She will only help with the birthing of our baby.

She left. At the same moment, I started hearing my mother groaning very quietly. She groaned and groaned and groaned. I covered my ears with the pillow and I left my eyes half-opened, filled with tears, as I awaited the arrival of my father and Madam Chica, who came in giving orders:

– Someone put water on the stove. Make a very hot royal pepper and mint tea.

13

My mother groaned and groaned. The day was passing by and there I was, forgotten. No one remembered that I could be hungry or thirsty, not even I. The sun with its tired rays was shining through the window linings when I could no longer help myself and knelt down beside the bed and started praying:

– My Our Lady of my mother's prayers, do not let her cry; I will never again curse the devilish and trashy baby secretly in my heart. If she stops groaning, from now onwards, I will only sing Little Jesus for him. Amen.

I made the sign of the cross and as I was getting back in bed to continue my vigil, the groans stopped. Abruptly, a baby's strong cry was heard throughout the house, even in my own room. Jesus was being born.

The following day my mother started receiving visitors. Everyone in the neighborhood came with presents for the baby. They seized the opportunity to thank my mother for helping them cure all of their children's sicknesses, including roundworm, upset stomach, or even evil eye. They brought fat, yellow, white, and striped hens. As Madam Jandira explained to Iraci, they did not bring black hens because they are very hard and are only used for sacrificial rituals.

Every day, as early as possible, many women came. They brought bathing soap, talcum, and meters of textiles for the baby's clothes. I did not even pay attention to them. I sat on the pavement of the house entrance, totally indifferent. But they always had something to tell me: "What a pity, the pampering is over!" Others would say: "I'll take him with me." "You can all go to …," I would say to myself, and then I would regret and make the sign of the cross.

My mother would occasionally see visitors to the door. On such occasions, she would grab my hand and say:

> – Let's go to the room to see your little brother. Mother cannot bring him here before seven days have passed. He could catch the seven-day bad omen. And there is no cure for that. Let's go my daughter, let's go...

I never went. Let him stay there and take my place. I did not go. I would meet him on the eight day, after the period of catching any disease was past, when my mother would bring him out of her room. I really could not care less either way. I only felt some relief when I no longer had to call him Little Jesus.

He was black.

Lonesome Voices

With the arrival of Zezinho, everything changed around the house. Cecília no longer went to work at the laundry place. She stayed to help out at home. She cooked for everyone: those of us at home and those struggling in the countryside. Complete confusion. Organizing and cleaning the house, making meals, and washing the clothes. Beyond all that, Zezinho's baths, Zezinho's cups of tea, Zezinho's diapers, Zezinho's cries. Zezinho: every minute, every hour, every day, always.

Cema seemed to have foreseen things. He started operating like a rainbow. He scattered things on the floor, disorganized the chairs, climbed the table, ate the earth that seemed like excretion: peed and defecated every five minutes.

They decided to prioritize the household chores. Cecília would wash all the clothes and keep an eye on Cema. My mother would make the meals and would attend to Zezinho's impudence. Whoever has any time remaining would clean the house. The rest of the individual attention will be focused on me, who was not too demanding. Food after; bath after. Everything after everything.

- You are a big girl; you can wait to take your shower.
- You are a grown girl, wait a little to have your lunch.

Just by sheer insolence, I lost all desire and hunger. I only felt like sleeping. I felt cold all all the time, day and night. Cold whether it was raining or sunny. In every circumstance, always cold.

> – Roundworm, Madam Chica said, which caused heart-aching during routine household affairs.

Roundworm, my tail! I was suffering more from nostalgia than anything. Nostalgia of my lost special privileges. The warmth of being carried on my mother's neck; of someone serving my food and helping me eat; of being able to ask silly questions; of attracting affectionate eyes. Memory of my mother saying: "peel an orange for my daughter; I will take care of combing her hair; give her a comforter so she does not get cold." Roundworm, just like the nose of Madam Chica. It was nostalgia for sure. Yet, nostalgia is never cured with cups of tea.

One day, I was asleep, following the movement of a small spider which was going zigzag on the roof, when I heard my mother praying on the other side of the wall:

> – Our Lady of Aparecida, you are a mother just like me, come to answer my prayers. Pour your powerful blessings on my daughter; let her get better through the love of God. Relieve us of our sufferings so we can return to being a happy family again. In the name of the Father, the Son, and the Holy Ghost, Amen.

I felt a sharp pain in my heart. I never wanted nor did I think of causing my family any pain. I wish I could do something about the situation immediately. If I could, I would go to thank them, return the smiles of family members, eat, eat everyday and at all times.

As I was making efforts to get up, the door opened.

> – My daughter, Madam Pedrinha gave us a loaf of bread with lard. Here is a piece. Eat so you feel its delicacy. If you eat...

I forced myself to smile, and took the piece of bread. As I ate, she looked at me as if stupefied, almost chewing along with me. To take maximum advantage of the moment of enchantment, I quickly swallowed the piece and asked for another.

— You want more? Let me fetch more. Blessed be the name of Jesus.

She left and returned few seconds after. She came with Cecília, Zezinho wrapped around her neck, Cema, Iraci, Arminda, Dirceu, and my father, holding on to his hoe still. All of them surrounded me. Some sat on the bed while others knelt anywhere they freely could. They were happy to watch me eat, without any moment of silence in the exaggerated vigil. Then my father signaled to my mother and said:

— Tomorrow for sure, you will go to town to buy a candle, in order to pay your pledge.

He put his working hoe on his neck, and left whistling.

— Do you want more? Iraci asked.

Before I could reply, Arminda burst into sarcasm:

— We also would not want to fatten the little girl once and for all.

Everyone laughed aloud because the occasion was funny. I also laughed, and taking advantage of the flashing moment, I placed my head on my mother's bosom. All her clothing was wet with milk. Her chest, all heavy, was leaking of

milk. Discretely, I used my index finger to feel the liquid, smelled it, and licked it.

Really, that milk was meant for Zezinho. It was not the motherly milk I was used to.

Affinities: Eyes Within

- Did you see that? Even he liked it. – It was the little spider still moving zigzag on the roof.
- What do you think; I already know. But what did you all say... He who?
- Your little brother.
- He liked it? I did not realize it.
- Of course. You never realize when others like something. Better still, you do, but you would rather they like things your own way. Every one.
- He never paid attention to me. Of this, at least, I am sure. It is not a lie.
- What about you? Have you ever paid any attention to me?
- Me?
- Of course. You never paid attention to me and I live here.
- I did not even realize it. I am so sorry.
- Now you understand? You are the kind of person not to bother with others. I am not referring to your naked eyes of looking at others but the eyes within.
- I understand. But I always thought that people and animals are not sensitive to those yours you are referring to. Not that I want to be as sensitive as animals are, you know. I am not suggesting that. Well, let me not get into that right now. It is a long story. Now then, from now on, I will pay attention

to him and you. But he does not know how to play. What about you, do you know any better? Play with what?
- Everyone knows how to play. Even the older ones. I play with so much stuff! For example, looking at others, speaking with children, laughing with others; you know what I am talking about.
- I do. I never thought you were this smart. You have just taught me many things about looking, about paying attention to others.

The little spider moved around.

- I have enjoyed the talk but I need to go.
- You want to leave now that we are...
- No, I am not leaving. I am not leaving once and for all. Didn't I say I that live here?
- I had even forgotten all that.

Zezinho cried in the other room. I looked at my friend, somewhat undecided; but her smart self helped me out.

- Go ahead. Would you like to...

I left, running.

He was naked, jumpy, and kicking. I lifted him up and held him within my hands. He stopped acting out and silently enjoyed my affection.

- I thought you never cared about me. May God forgive me; I even thought, perhaps, that you were blind within. Sorry. I have always been somewhat silly. But from now on, I will no longer be sad if my older siblings have no time for me. I will always

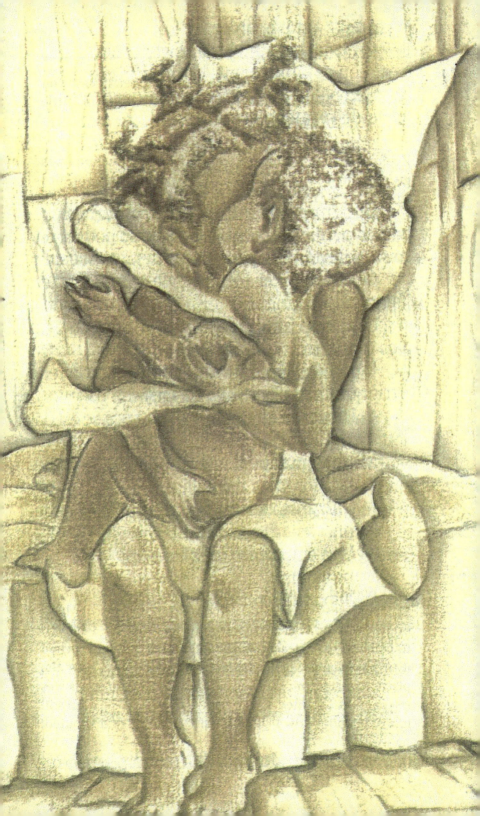

speak with you or with my little spider, in case you are sleeping. If you also need to talk to my little spider, please feel free to do so.

Zezinho opened his mouth and enjoyed the affection I was giving him. He smiled. His weak breathing came alive once again, as if for the first time.

How nice it is to have friends. Not those close friends with whom I could only share intimate ideas so as not to be embarrassed. What is more exciting is the fulfillment that voices and attitudes engender. Being able to speak my mind, get responses to everything, and believe that everything is possible, in an open and simple world.

One day, I wanted to know who could have made the door latch of the door to the moon.

— Psssiu! I called out. — Where are you hiding?

My little spider did not respond nor did it move around.

— I don't like this dirty game. You know. None of it.
— I am going to count to three: one, two, three. No movement whatsoever. I was scared. With my sharp eyes, I looked all over the place. Nowhere to be found.

I opened the door and found it at the door post, so small, faceless, legless, dry, my poor spider. Just its little body, torn to pieces on the wood. I was startled. I wanted to pick it up to at least open its inner eyes but as I touched it, it became powdery and the wind blew it all over the place. I started to cry. That did not help. My sadness was irreparable. I wanted to kill myself but could not. I am still ignorant about how I could possibly kill myself. I shouted:

- Zezinho! Zezinho!

I stopped calling because I remembered that he was not around. He had gone with my mother to borrow whatever from Madam Ernestina.

I left the room and sat on the stairs expecting him to ask for help. But when he came, I remembered that he could not communicate his feelings anyway. The young chap is weak; that much I knew. While waiting for the right time, I was overwhelmed by a terrible doubt.

- Zezinho, do you think that there is a spider type food in heaven?

He did not answer and I excused him in silence.

- Do you think that human heaven is bigger than that for animals?

Once again, he did not answer me and I also excused him in silence.

- Is it God who puts pounded ruby on people's ailments, or does He send Saint Peter or any other Saints to put it on?
- Gosh! I don't know, he responded without looking at me.

He took his paper parrot and left hurriedly. I noticed that his internal eyes, like other people's eyes, were now looking in a different direction.

Squints, if they go in a different direction and leave me alone, from then on, orphan of affinity and belief. Zezinho got mixed up in the foolishness of men, who naturally

did not give me any opportunity to catch up with them even if I tried to take longer steps. Whenever I asked what color the sky was, they stated the obvious: beautiful, big, and blue, etc. They did not understand that I wanted to know of the inner sky. I wanted the juice because the shell is more visible. That was why I decided only to maintain contact with people when it was necessary.

Contrary to human behavior, animals are friendlier and are more coherent. I learned to speak with them. I imitated every bird in the region. I completely understood the messages of dogs, cats, horses, ants, cockroaches, etc. When in order to smile I imitate the dog-collar jingles, and in order to ask for something, I sound like a cat, people started to look at me as crazy. That was why they put a crucifix on my neck, as advised by the local priest. They taught me "our father who art in heaven" as well as "thy will be done." I fulfilled all their wishes to the best of my understanding.

One day, at my mother's request, I went briefly to the farm to pick up cabbage for dinner. It so happened that when I arrived there, I found a long queue of ants, carrying a dead cockroach. I was terribly grieved. Nothing hurts more than the pain of one's friends and relatives. How would the children, mother, husband, and wife feel? I thought it better not to show my pain and solidarity. I deferred my feelings until the funeral. Bitter and depressed, I followed the dead cockroach to its final resting place.

I'm not sure of how much time I lost, but when I arrived at home, it was already very dark and my family was worried about my lateness. Faced with the ambience of everyone's apprehension, I quickly started explaining:

— Nothing really was the matter. I only accompanied the burial of the cockroach.

There was a complete silence. By the countenance on everyone's face, I realized that there must be something worse than my lateness. Or, could it be that I did not explain adequately? I decided to make myself better understood. I started barking like a dog uncontrollably. Contrary to what I expected, my mother started to cry. This was how I was taken to Madam Espanhola's house in the evening of the same day. After she made various strange gesticulations, she declared:

– You must bring the little girl here for nine days straight. She has been possessed. Zumbi's spirit is on her right side. I will prepare a special treatment. I will send off the evil spirit and request the protection of Saint Izildina.

That night, I slept with my right side against the thatched mattress. I was dozing and waking up intermittently. If this evil thing is unable to stay on my right side, would it reach for my back? As I returned to my restless sleep, I saw the prayer altar with lighted candles, innumerable prayer pamphlets, and images of a thousand saints which have been given the responsibility of protecting me. From that moment on, I pretended not to be in pain and minimized my groans so as not to worsen my condition.

Never again did I "walk like a toad," but I was certain that I had some kind of spiritual attack. I no longer spoke with animals—I could not—but the desire was always there.

It was during this same period that I caught the jigger worm on my foot. I was so very happy. The only problem was that I could not tell anyone; not even my mother, because once she finds out that any one of us had such a worm, she would use a pin, heated at the point, and insert it into the infected foot until the worm was removed. But I

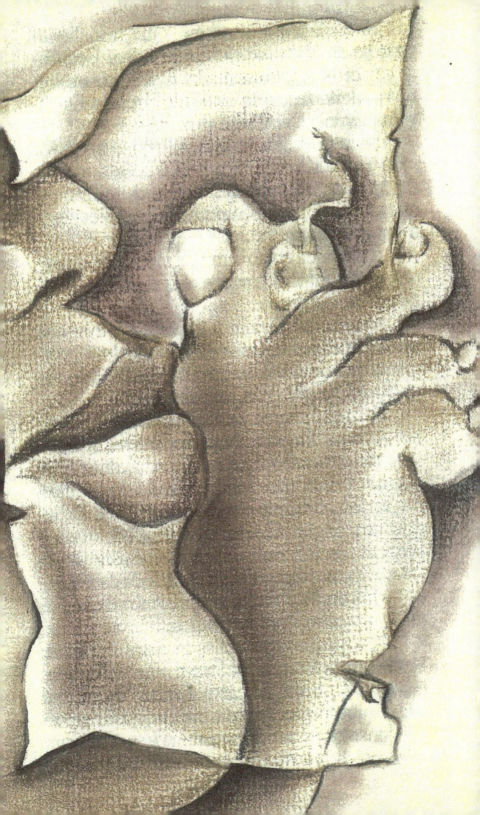

was no longer alone. My beloved worm kept me company and we carried on long dialogues.

I passed on my sadness and joy to it. There was an internal link that transported my thoughts to its house, at the very corner of my foot. From that corner came a delightful itching, bringing me answers and consolations. Our thoughts connected whether we were laughing or crying. One day, after so much happiness following affectionate lovemaking, I could not resist. I picked up a piece of calendar paper with the image of a supple big dog with its tongue hanging out. Through this dog, I sent messages to other friends:

– Please, let everyone know that I am very, very, happy indeed. I was infected by a beautiful worm on my foot. Let them know that I have no hard feelings towards anyone. The Zumbi spirit—I made a sign of the cross—is persecuting me and could also pursue them. I swear that I'd never, never, forgotten anyone. When the evil spirit departs and Saint Izildina arrives, I will let her know. For now, bye-bye. Sleep well.

Journeys

Unappealing life, I started to plan. Moving on with my life; getting out of the household. Not thinking of going too far from my parents and siblings, though. But to any kind of tree, move in with any John Doe; or maybe with a poultry owner and live with our roasted chicken. I could gain some weight or lose some.

I was lost within myself. In these lonely conversations with myself, I saw the unlikelihood of realizing such a dream. How could I possibly explain this to my mother and get the approval of my family? The worst that could happen is deal with Madam Chica; drink cups and more cups of tea. See my mother cry again all over the place and I, head-bowed, looking pitiful, crazy, and without any solution.

I put my plans in action. It was just a matter of dying on the side of the living. I alienated myself in order to re-integrate myself within the context. I struck close friendship with all the kids of the Colony. I wanted to learn how to cry for a doll, laugh aloud, walk within the thighs of adults, cry for menthol candies. I geared myself up for anything. Animals; don't even think about them. I even laughed when a silly kid kicked a stray dog sleeping on the road that she was passing through. I stopped being a problem or creating one. I became like the Joneses: who went anywhere with everyone. One day, I discovered a way of pleasing myself while playing the game of acceptance at the same time.

In front of Madam Ernestina's house was an enormous silk-cotton tree. Everyone liked it. It was used for all kinds of playful things. When sun was setting and it was refresh-

ingly cool, boys made bird-traps and constructed paper parrots. The girls created a balancing act to see who could last longer on their toes under the swinging cord.

- Let's see who could last longer?
- I go first.
- I go second, someone else would answer.

They keep balancing the ups and downs, adjusting their thighs, arms, and the chord, accordingly; creating a pleasant game.

I waited for my turn. I was not in a hurry. I was not even worried if I was last. While I was balancing, I would travel to places that my playmates could not even imagine existed or that they could not possibly get to know. How often did I travel to São Paulo, Rio de Janeiro, Bahia, Minas? But I went and returned quickly, within the limits allowed by the balancing game. It has been a while that I have considered the idea of going to Santos because I heard the nurse taking care of my mother tell of his experience and say that it was all marvelous. He described buildings and streets. He talked about the endless sea that and the feeling of standing on top of the world at the seashore.

He told of how folks bathed in the salty waters, and later rested by the seaside to dry off in the sun. For all these reasons, I wanted to go to Santos. The journey was going to be difficult, however, because it would not make sense to just force my way. I did not want to go for going's sake only and then regret it. I would rather go when the time was right. I wanted to step on the beach sand, wet my body, taste the salty waters, and anything else that may be unexpected.

I thought of the possibility of going to the Tree Station alone but the folkloric one-legged monster (Saci) is terrible. He would come through the whirlwind to steal children from their mothers and disappear with them. He would take children to the mountains where they were fed with mud and as for quenching their thirst, they made do with drops of dew from the corn leaves. Two days ago, two children had disappeared. In town: daughter of João Pedro Boiadeiro from the Quebra-Pote farm, and in Creonice neighborhood, daughter of Madam Maria Mulata, who lived in Palmeiras. But one day, when I least expected it, we found a solution.

– Whoever let me swing on the balance today can have my twenty and twenty of the other player, then and then can keep taking mine. That would mean three days of play and who goes along can have so many days of swinging.

Many kids went along with the idea; they have never gotten such a good deal before. I struck an agreement with Neide.

I sat on the swing and started my journey. I closed my eyes to see the trajectory even better. All of a sudden, I found myself in downtown. I saw the building where folks smiled like rich people through their fancy windows and makeshift gardens.

I was becoming hungry and I stopped to have some snacks. I ate bread and jam and drank sugar cane juice. I did not want to drink anything I was used to already such as a soda drink. I rested a little and continued towards the beach. I almost put my feet in the water when I remembered that it was not prudent to swim with a heavy stomach. I sat instead.

I breathed profoundly to invite the sea. It looked towards me quite indifferently. I thought and thought. Then I felt like indulging myself. I walked sluggishly, tiredly, and reluctantly. I was somewhat afraid. So many mysteries in their immensity; so much magic in their leg-

endary dimensions! So much perfection and suppleness in its self-submission to the earth that which it has taken from the earth! But it finally came, it was humbling and strengthening. With close affinities, I took all the liberties in the world.

– Pleased to meet you. I am enjoying you.
– The pleasure is ...

Suddenly, a wave lifted me and threw me far away from the beach.

– What a rogue! You gave twenty, then twenty, and one more. Black doll, fake hairdo! You can go to hell! – That was Neide complaining about my not honoring my agreement.

All of them started cursing me un-empathically, asking me to leave. I started crying profusely. "Black doll, fake hairdo" were the common insults. Alright! What then do I do with the sea awaiting me with its anxious mouth? What do I do with the words that are locked up in my creative master's throat?

There was no point in my trying to argue. They did not allow me to return to the beach, and even if they allowed me, I would not know how to ask the sea to pardon my friends' lack of home training. I went home sobbing, thinking that Saci was not as bad he has been portrayed. Perhaps he was a misunderstood figure, and hopefully with some explanation, he may let me stay alone by the tree and not take me anywhere as he usually does. I would not hurt him, nor would he hurt me. Without such ill-will of Saci, I could travel. I always believed in the possibility of agreements, especially when people take time to dialogue.

Amidst these reflections, I arrived at home to find my mother rumbling through a dress of hers where she normally kept documents. In order to hide my interest in something that I have not been invited to be part of, I asked:

- What are you looking for?
- Your birth certificate. A young lady came here looking for names of children who are seven year old. You are going to be. Where have you been all the while?
- At the sea... having fun with everyone. And when do I start school?
- We give them your name now but you start only next year.
- Who else will start school next year?
- All children who are about your age: Toninho, Flávio, Ana. Many children.
- What if Flávio calls me a nigger on the way?
- I do not want to hear of any foolishness, for God's sake! If that happens, pretend that you did not hear anything.

I kept quiet. Who am I to say that I am already fed up? My mother found the so-called birth certificate and came over to show me.

- Here it is.

She smiled with relief and in turn, pretending: I also smiled.

School Days

My mother braided my hair. Sitting on a seat that my father had put together with left over wood from the pounder, which while still new, was used as a corn grinder for the chicken, while I, with so much curiosity, would stand in front of him, hearing the pounding silently.

- Tomorrow, your hair will be ready. Today, you will seep with a scarf on your head so as not to disentangle everything. Don't forget to put the new bed sheet on the bed. For God's sake, don't forget your bleeding nose. Wash your face before leaving the house.
- If we end up leaving anyway, what would the teacher do? – I asked.
- You will be punished by being asked to kneel on two corn seeds – she answered me.
- But Janete, daughter of Mr. Cardoso usually goes with starry-eyed face and mucous-filled nose and...
- But Janete is white – my mother answered before I could complete my sentence.
- Still on this matter, I heard my father interject from the kitchen:
- Come on in, Madam Rosária. – And then even louder:
- Bastiana, Madam Rosária has arrived.

Madam Rosária was an old black woman who used to live in the other farm with a family of farmers. No one knew why she lived with that family nor does anyone know her actual age. Some say she is 98, others say 112. Whenever she is asked, she answered somewhat discreetly:

- Only my son knows.
- And where is your son? – Others would probe further.

But instead, she, already upset, would simply murmur:

- Gosh! (Ué), Mr. Pedro João, don't you know?
- Owner of the farm?
- Of course. – She would answer.

Then, she would shut down her face; and no one else was crazy enough to dare to probe any further for the fear that she would be afraid and would no longer tell us stories about slavery. The truth is that when Grandma Rosária—so we called her—would arrive, she came with all the children. Everyone wanted to hear her tell those beautiful and sad stories. So it was on a given day, that Grandma Rosária sat, almost pushed over by a little girl, my mother quickly tidied my hair so that we could sit with her and hear her stories.

When we arrived, she was saying:

- and it was only with a signature on paper that the whole population was set free from slavery. Some went out dancing and singing. Others, still retained by a disobedient master, only sang. There was also a lot of circular drinking for anyone who wanted it.
- Who? – I asked Lilico quietly, who has been following the story from the very beginning.
- Some Princess Isabel. Be quiet!

Grandma Rosária continued. She either spoke emphatically or quietly with emotions but we needed to pay close attention in order to understand her. On occasions, I could no longer follow and I asked questions:

— Grandma Rosária, was she a Saint?

But she was already sleeping on her seat, at which point the kids would start to get up and leave. Nevertheless, I always got an answer:

— She could only be, my daughter — my father said.
— The purest and most honest — my mother added.
— "She could only be," I thought.

Since I have already allowed Grandma Rosária to pass, my mother went towards her room. I also went to my room and lit a candle. I prayed, saying three "Our Fathers" and three "Ave Marias." I appealed to Saint Princesa Isabela to help me not to forget my wake up time or to clean my dirty nose. I also thanked her for being so nice to the slaves. I slept, formulating some poetic lines in my head. When I could read and write — she would help me — and I would write on paper so as to recite the poems in school.

Just when my eyes were responding to the charm of the candle, and the poetic lines were about to come to fruition, my mother called me.

— Daughter, wake up, for it is time.

She did not even need to call me. I never slept.
I got up from bed.
... Our Father who art in heaven...

- Did you pick up your handkerchief?

... blessed be Your name...

- Don't fight with Flávio on the way; afterwards, his father will tell Mariano. Weak folks always get blamed for things and your father does not like being involved in such matters.

... so let it be on earth as in heaven. Virgin Mary, mother of God...

My mother was giving the run-around. Blue skirt, white blouse. New socks for my feet. Rice powder all over my body. Clean nose. I was a black girl ... Janete is white, now and until we die. Suddenly, I heard some joyful noise coming from outside into the house. Children of the community were having a party. We were going to school. Someone called me.

- Geniiiiii... ... amen ...
- Bless you mother. God be with you.
- God bless you. God be with you too.

Don't lose your handkerchief. Don't fight with Flávio so as not to... The rest of the don'ts were noted as I joined other kids and stayed away from trouble.

- I will kiss my teacher on the way out of school.
- Tell Diva that she is already in the second year.
- I'll also kiss the teacher – Arminda said.
- I always kiss all of them – said Iraci, the veteran student, who is now more experienced because she has passed to fourth year.
- Must everyone kiss the teachers? I asked.
- Of course, everyone does – Diva answered.

- No such thing – Iraci countered. – Whoever wants to kiss, kisses. Who does not want to, needs not do so.
- I will not kiss any damn teacher! – Dirceu, a terrible black girl, who managed to pass to third year, shouted.

I did not bother myself with Dirceu's answer as she was getting somewhat very skeptical. What would I do? Kiss or not kiss? Should I or shouldn't I? Would I have the courage to do so? And if I didn't, what would happen? I was worried all the time in class. I was looking for either reasons to kiss or excuses not to do so.

- Well – the teacher said. – Now, the break is over. I think all of you know what a snake is, right? Well, then, let's draw some real snakes.

I felt like telling her that my mother knew how to cure snake bites. Then one day... Oh my God, I would not have the courage to interrupt her. Besides, she would know the same thing. She was a teacher after all. Madam Odete started drawing headless snakes on the board, while taking crazy breaks in-between. Perhaps blind snakes are headless. I think these ones are blind snakes.

- "This must be the case," I thought.

And what is the matter with those snake heads; why were they so twisted? Perhaps she does not know how to draw snake heads properly?
My God, should I kiss or not kiss?

- Why did you do so?

I pulled a desk. My heart started pumping fast.

- Explain, come on! – She cried out loud. – Look, here is his. – She took the notebook of a boy sitting on the desk on her side and flashed it in my face. All is well. Why did you not draw it right?
- The snake ... – I was trying to explain. Tears started rolling down my cheeks and the cries overwhelmed me to the point of losing my voice. Suddenly, a striking bell rang powerfully. The kids gathered together. It was the signal that classes were over for that day. I could not stop crying. My nose started running. I cleaned the mess with the tip of my blouse. My handkerchief, my God, where did I even put it? Why was my tear salty and the nose mucus not?

"I think our mothers put salt in our eyes when we sleep," I thought.

No. It couldn't possibly be. Our eyes would have hardened, for sure. I quickly collected my notebooks at once. I felt an elbow push on my back. It was Diva letting me know:

- I have already given a kiss. Iraci and Laurinha as well. Go, hurry up. New sense of panting and hoarse voice. The kiss! There was no time for doubts. I was the only one left.

I got up quickly; I adjusted my legs and took aim at the teacher's face. I took two steps towards the door; I stumbled against the desk but kept going. Madam Odete, using her back hands, cleaned the mess I had in advertently left on her face. I could then see her palm. She was white, very white. It felt like the pigeon's wing which always hung around the roof of Madam Neide's house. Is it a pigeon's wing that is the hand or the hand that is a wing? I walked home all by myself. The other kids had gone home together; walking very fast, while I was walking slowly without realizing it.

At some point, I saw my mother, who was waiting for me along the way.

- Everyone has arrived, daughter. Don't delay any more. I left bread in the oven...
- Mother, are there headless snakes?
- There you go again with those silly questions of yours. Of course; there is no such thing. Why do you ask?
- Because...

I started crying again. I sobbed. I started having headaches. My belly was aching. She picked me up on her shoulder, and with the tip of her clothes, wiped away my tears. I fell asleep on her back as I tried to explain my nameless pain:

- I am crying because I am hungry.

Metamorphosis

The following year, on the very first day of classes, I was carrying a four-line poem in my bag which went like this:

> Was great for the slaves
> Like honey it seemed
> Sister of God I thought she was
> Long Live Princess Isabel.

At first, I lacked the courage to show it to the teacher. Every time I tried, I was frozen and my heart was almost jumping out of me. But the following day, when she complimented me that my writing was great, I took out the poem and gave it to her. She went to her table and sat with my paper in her hand. She read and re-read it. She took her pen and corrected a few things in my poem and sent Pedro to fetch the Director. Immediately, I felt like peeing and vomiting. Could it be that I have done something wrong? And if that is the case, am I going to be punished by kneeling on corn seeds?

The director arrived followed by Pedro. Madam Cacilda gave him the paper. The director read it. They spent some time discussing and referring to something I had written. Afterwards, he left the room and the teacher continued teaching calmly, without any indication of whether she liked the poem or not. But with every remote noise, I was so perplexed and anxious for any kind of signal or explanation, however banal it might sound.

So I felt until the end of classes but as my group was passing through the doorway of the Director's office, the director came out looking for me with some curious countenance, saying:

- Congratulations.
- It was nothing. Thank you.

I went home quite happy. Like roosted song-thrush birds overcoming the odds, I felt on top of the world.

It must have been May 10 or 11. Shortly after the break, Madam Cacilda told us:

- On May 13, we are now going to have a party for Princess Isabel who freed the slaves. Who wants to recite a poem?

Many kids shouted: --

- I! I! I!

Puff, Puff... there goes my heart again pumping so fast to the extent of suffocating my voice. It was the time and place to share my poem with everyone. I could not miss the opportunity. But how was I going to mobilize the courage? What if I made a mistake?

- Don't be so timid! – The teacher scolded. – Raise up your hands.
- I raised mine, which was like negritude amongst other white and pale hands.
- You... You... You...

I was not selected. We could select only so many, she explained. But I could not afford to miss the opportunity. I ran after her, panting.

– Madam Cacilda, I have that poem that I wrote the other day, which I showed to you; and you showed to the director and he even commended me and I left it...

I rushed through everything I wanted to say without any perspiration. Without any break. Fear of not convincing her, of closing my eyes and tears would flow uncontrollably, full of emotions. I was saturated.

– Fine. Tomorrow, you can bring the poem and we will practice.

She cleared my face and laughed sparingly. Her hands felt like a hen's feet and her lips, even with her smile, looked like those tomato peels that my mother used as rice seasoning. I went home somewhat anguished. I almost regretted having insisted. Reading and memorizing the poem was not the problem. The challenge would be not crying or going blank through anxiety at the moment of reading.

I thought of not going to school for a few days, coming up with some excuse like stomach ache, but I could not forget someone like Princess Isabel. She deserved it. If not for her.... Which sin would be greater: lie that I was sick or not pay homage to Saint Princess Isabel?

I decided to go and not sin. Better to be nervous and to cry than to be punished by God. Punished by God or Princess Isabel? By both, of course. She would need to ask for His consent to punish me since He is the Father, Boss, and master of all decisions. Is there really a meeting in heaven among saints and angels? Oh no. Children are not

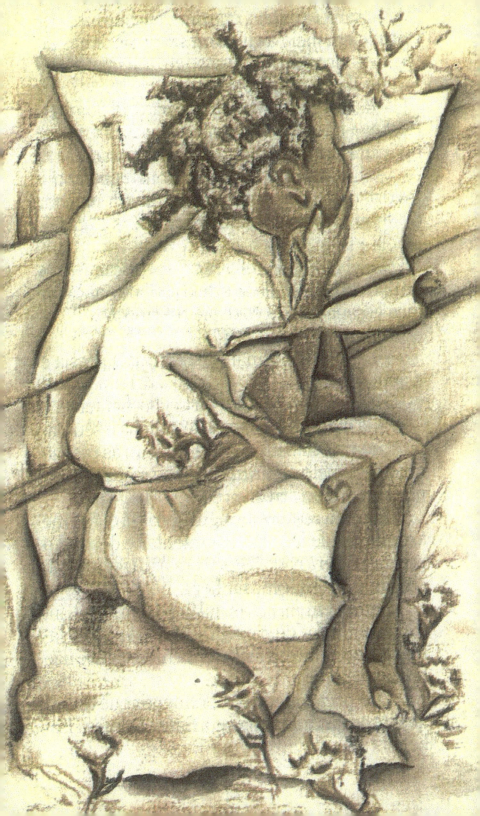

supposed to have opinions, they don't decide anything. They don't even vote. Oh, if they only could vote... If they could, things would be easier. I also knew different angels: Tilica 1, who died from ringworm, Luzia 2, who died from stomach upset, Jorge 3, who died from falling into the well.

Yes, indeed. And there was many more still, who, incidentally, are of my same black color. These would have been votes in my favor, for sure. Except for Ana, who was white, João Cláudio... I think even they...but there is no point in thinking these things. A child only listens, when he or she can.

The fact is that in heaven everyone will find out. A terrible shame overwhelmed me, just like the day I was caught while trying to find out how an egg enters into the belly of a hen. Goodness! There was really no alternative. It was a matter of taking responsibility once and for all, trying to do everything right and well. I ate my lunch quickly. I swallowed almost everything. I forced myself to write whatever. I persisted. I created four new lines.

> Stubborn were men
> Anger was their controller
> Hence Princess Isabel
> Let loose all tha' slaves.

I read the previous lines I had written all over and felt they should come at the end; so as to end the declamation with "Long live Princess Isabel." I gave my poem another title: "Saint Isabel." It then became:

> "Saint Isabel"
> Stubborn were men
> Anger was their controller
> Hence Princess Isabel
> Let loose all tha' slaves.

> Was great for the slaves
> Like honey it seemed
> Sister of God I thought she was
> Long Live Princess Isabel.

Within a half an hour, I had memorized everything. Then I started reciting slowly. At times, I started from the end and returned to the beginning. Everything was perfect. Not even a slight stammering, no single word missed; nothing.

The following day, I left my poem on the table for the teacher to see. She picked it up, read it and made some spelling changes, such as pluralizing "men" in "man," and making adjustments in adjectival agreements, etc. She returned it to me.

– Memorize it because tomorrow, you will be reciting it, alright?

I was not bothered because I had already memorized everything to the last word.

The party was planned for the following day, after the break. But as soon as we entered the classroom, the teacher started speaking about the date:

– Today we celebrate the liberation of slaves. Slaves were blacks that came from Africa. Here they were forced to work and they were not paid for all the work they performed. They were tied to tree trunks and at times, beaten to death. When ...

She continued discussing the issue for about fifteen minutes. I realized that her narrative was different from the one told by Grandma Rosária. Africans were good, simple, human, religious. They were stupid, cowardly, and imbecile. They did not react to punishment, never defended themselves, at least. When it was my turn, the whole class looked at me with sympathy and sarcasm. I was the only one in class representing a race full of compassion! I wanted to disappear but could not. All I could do was to ask for permission to go to the bathroom. Sitting on the toilet, I used my index finger to write "Lazarus-like" in the air. That was not enough. I continued: "morphetic." I accented the "e" and went back to class.

During the break, Sueli came to give an apple and Raquel, daughter of the Farm's administrator, offered to trade her lunch with mine. I did not eat it, of course. It was not worth it. Her lunch was not like spilled milk that one could easily pass a napkin over and it was clean. Instead, it was like blood. Who could make it up? Life? Let the fine river flow calmly. But how could one reclaim it from within, where the open wound was my personal silence, an incomparable pain?

During the ceremony, there was a glitch. Meanwhile, I did not worry about what went wrong or right, successes or failures. I was overwhelmed with shame. I thought I was the greatest of them all because I was the only one to write a poem. I wondered how many times they must have made fun of me, after all my craziness of coming up with group songs. I was made to believe that I came from a passive race, without history, or histories of heroism. They were dying just like dogs. But it was commonplace to pay homage to Caxias, Tirandentes and all the Dom Pedros of history. Sure enough. They fought, defended their nation. As for the black idiots, they did nothing.

This was why my father was so fearful of Mr. Godói, the administrator, and my mother taught us not to fight with Flávio. A black man is said to be weak. Even my father and mother. This is why I was afraid of everything. A child pushed his father, who pushed his grandfather, who pushed.... Resultantly, even my foolish self became part of

the same line of thought. I felt lost within myself when I heard the teacher commenting:

- You forgot? Not to worry. Next ceremony, you can recite. Soon after came the Day of Anchieta, the soldier.... Let's sit. It is not important.

She took me calmly to a seat around other teachers in front. I was feeling sleepy and thirsty. I felt it strange that I was so calm and peaceful. I felt something all over my neck. I wanted to check if the pain was in the chest, but I restrained myself. "Is he dead?" To hell! If he wants to die, let him die," I thought, looking at the stuff coming out of the nose slowly and spreading all over my new skirt. That day, no one was running on the way home. Everyone surrounded me because they were worried that I could not walk any faster. I felt almost weightless and as if every step I took was a step backward. When I arrived home, my mother said:

- Your food is on top of the stove. After, you take the plate to the washing sink as I already leaving to wash the trains.

I got rid of my school materials and picked up my food. I was about going to toss the food to the chicken when I thought, if I should go that soon, my mother would suspect me for no one ate that fast. I decided to wait a while longer. I started stirring the food for no reason. I separated the black bean seeds with the tip of the spoon; throwing them in the middle of the flame on the stove. Afterwards, I threw all the food away in the garden and took the plate to where my mother had instructed.

At that time, women of our rural zone did not know the "thousand and one functions of a bright pot-cleaner;"

in order to clean utensils, they would grind tiles and use the powder to clean utensils. The idea came to me when I saw my mother try to clean accumulated coal at the bottom of the pot. As soon as she finished cleaning, she came inside and I gathered the rest of the powder and rubbed it against my black stomach. Despite the pain it caused, I continued rubbing. Eventually, I realized that it was impossible to remove blackness from one's skin. I was left with a raw, bloody patch of skin of my abdomen. I started using the blood to write pornographic words on the wall of the water tank.

When I arrived at home, my mother, seeing my all skin grazed and bloody, left what she was doing and went to look for some leaves to soothe my wounds. While I was feeling better, she would take a wrapper to cover my legs, saying:

- Lord, have mercy! I am tired of talking: don't jump the walls, don't run while playing; and yet this! It goes in through one ear and goes out through the other. You are like a rascal. What a lie! Not even a rascal behaves this way. Look at Zezinho; he wouldn't...

I heard her voice from a distance; bragging, somewhat lively. Within a week, only some markings were left over; an ample proof of my own violence against myself. The scourge of the soul will continue to hope for healing which only time and human justice could render.

Foundation

My father arrived home from his laborer's job, removed the empty coffee carafe from the strap on his shoulder, and sat on the stairs by the kitchen door. He asked me to fetch his roll of tobacco leaves with which he customarily prepared his cigarettes for the next day or two while waiting for dinner. I brought it to him and as he opened it, his face lit up like a Pelé smiling in front of a news magazine. As he was disentangling the wrapper to see the contents even better, he said to me:

- Yes, this one was lucky. Read the content for me, my daughter. Speak slowly; otherwise, I won't be able to follow you.

I picked up the newspaper and started to read, including the sports sections which included information about the fantastic lives of players. There were many words whose meanings I could not decipher, but when I looked at my father's face, he would burst out laughing quite awkwardly without losing his grip on the tobacco. When I finished reading, he said:

- Thank God. You see now, my daughter? It was like that for us too. One's father was the one to feel the shame. Seeing one's child like this, we even sometimes forget about life's hardships.

He breathed very profoundly and continued:

— If we could at least each our own kids...

I felt so much pity for my father that I hardly dared to ask:

— Father, what could a woman study?
— She could be a seamstress, a teacher...— He forced a smile and appeared to want to end the conversation. — Let's stop dreaming.
— I am going to be a teacher — I said assuredly.

My father looked at me as if he had heard some blasphemies.

— Oh, if only that could come true, I won't mind dying at the hand of the hoe. — He looked at me somewhat consoled. — Of course, you never lacked the intelligence.
— Yes, father, I am going to be a teacher.

I wanted him to forget about the hardships of life.

When I started Junior High, I came home with my school materials under my arm, and he would be waiting for me at the beginning of the road, the main entrance to the town. On one of these days, we crossed a small farm and we talked about my studies:

— This is how it should be, my daughter. If we don't help ourselves, others are not going to do so.

At the same time, the administrator was passing by; while stopping to share a few words, he greeted my father and told him:

— I have nothing to do with this but you black people are made of iron. Your place is to work hard as

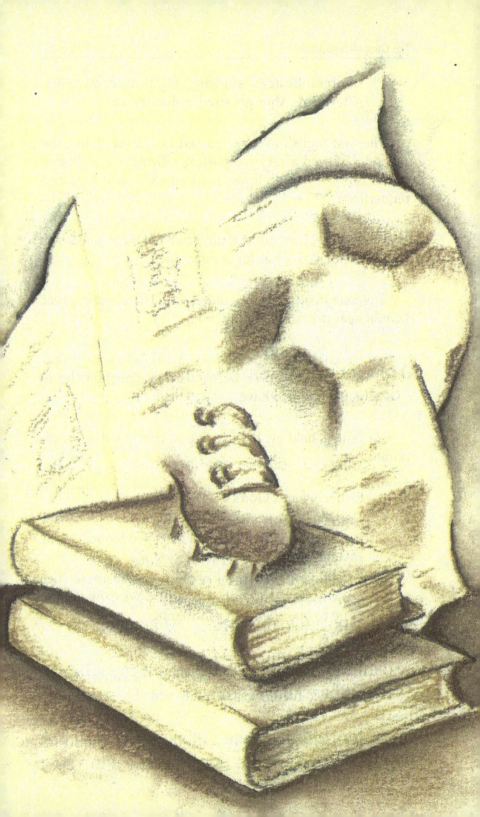

laborers. Besides, studying, my dear, is stupidity. Afterwards, they get tired and so do we...

The first foolish jive was passed unanswered, but the second deserved a very categorical, affirmative, and marvelous answer which almost made me die with love and tenderness:

— You see, I am not actually studying for myself — my father said — but for my daughter.

The man turned cold shoulders, and left so quietly that I could hear my father still talking:

— He could even be a white man. But more proud than I could ever be. A teacher daughter, he is never going to have.

He smiled, held my hands, and we continued our walk home.

— Father, what is God's color?
— Goodness (Ué)... White — he affirmed.
— But no one ever saw Him in flesh and blood. Could He not be black?
— Daughter of God, think about what you are saying. It is written in the Holy Scriptures. We cannot continue to blaspheme in this manner.
— But the Holy Scriptures...

He looked at me, seemingly irritated by the conversation, and because I could not insist, I only added:

– I mean if He is black, when He dies, you can replace Him. You are such a good man!

In my whole life, I have never seen my father laugh so much. He laughed wildly. He laughed until we arrived at home, and when my mother saw him so relaxed, she said to brothers:

– He must have seen a green bird, for sure.

Since he did not stop laughing, everyone went along and the mood was lively and happy. That was when I lost my composure and I took a wide step to give my mother a kiss in the belly. Everyone thought I was strange but also knew it was one of my overwhelmed moments. I was ashamed, and to cover up, I pretended to be removing something from within my inner teeth.

Becoming a Woman

- Mother, there is a growth here. I wonder if it is the pain-inflicting one? Every day, I feel a pinch.

She immediately left the big loaf of bread she was making, washed her hands, and came to me. She lifted up my blouse and felt the growth.

- It is not a wound.
- I thought it was. What could it be then?
- Not to worry. Just the way it is.

The conversation was over and I looked at her face wondering what the wound could be. There was no change in her expression, no sign of concern whatsoever. If it was something serious, she would have surely cried, send for my dad at work, do something. Since everything continued normally, I calmed myself down and trusted her wisdom.

But days went by and the soreness persisted instead of getting better. I returned to my initial worries. I sought the help and goodness of my sister Maria, who was spending some days with us, along with her children.

- Maria, what could it be?
- What?

— This unusual growth in my chest. My mother said it was nothing but it continues to hurt and every day, it grows bigger.

Maria looked at me unconcerned and said very patiently:

— Mother was right. It is nothing at all. — She laughed wildly. —All it is that milk is beginning to form in you. Soon, very soon, they will be as big as mine. Look here.

She pointed to her big breasts and I, feeling ashamed, crossed my arms on my chest to hide mine, which were still showing.

Since I was not carrying any kind of disease, for sure, I completely forgot about the growths. Days after, I started feeling some strange stomach pain in my Mathematics class. When I realized that I could not handle it, I was compelled to tell the director and asked to be allowed to go home. My mother knew just the right tea to make to end such pain.

I took to the streets, dizzy and anguished. When the pain increased, I stopped and waited for it to subside; afterwards, I continued my walk home—constantly dealing with the accursed pain. Already close to home, I felt something flowing within my thighs. "I think I must be peeing on myself," I thought. I stopped by the cane field to check. I checked my skirt and my underwear; my thighs were all covered with blood. I was scared. What could that be, my God? Why was so much blood flowing from the inside of me?

I had no doubts. This time, it was a very serious sickness, without any possibility of treatment. I left running. I felt like flying in order to arrive as quickly as possible.

The kitchen's door was slightly closed; with a single pull, I opened it. My mother was stirring something in the pot. She looked at me quite surprised, awaiting an explanation for my unusually aggressive posture.

> – Look mother, I think I must my cut everything in my vein. Help me!

She abandoned what she was cooking on the stove, and reluctantly, started explaining:

> – You became a woman, stupid. Everyone went through it. Arminda, Iraci, Maria, Cecília, even Cema and I went through it. This is how it works.

She stopped talking and waited for me to relax. She held my hand and set out for the Washer place where she got the household clothes washed. She removed all my clothes and put me under the tap water. She passed her hands all over my body and played with me saying:

> – Dramatic young woman, believe it! Now the game is over. You can no longer play with those rascals with your legs showing everything. You are no longer a kid. You have to behave like an adult. When we attain the age of...

She kept talking, and talking, and talking. I could see my young blood flowing slowly, mixed with the tap water and disappearing before my very eyes. My childhood was passing by, leaving me to be more careful, with no time to play around, one more game in the balance. I stayed there stupefied. A woman, as they now see me. Just a woman.

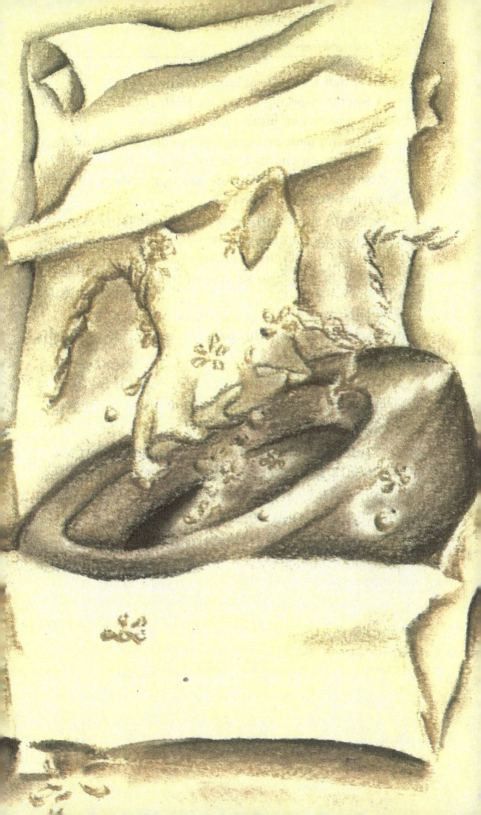

A woman, completing Junior High.

A woman, working on Senior High and on her way to becoming a teacher, fulfilling her dream.

A woman, figuring herself out under societal impositions; looking for energy to be strong.

A woman, laughing to hide her fear of the society, of life, of the pitfalls of her steps.

A woman, mastering her speech, joggling words, managing suburban jargon and the synonyms flowing freely from the tongue of refined urban society.

A woman, trying to survive in the midst of co-optations and prejudices.

A woman, everything and above all, right in front of the island: lies the monthly pad.

Crystal Moment

December was set for the realization of the ceremony. My graduation. At home, we discussed and decided that everyone was going to attend. We discussed what dress to wear and which shoes to put on—all befitting of the occasion. We evaluated things based on scarcity of money and came to terms with the following: we would only buy new items for me. Others would buy only what they lacked. For one we'd buy a dress, for another, shoes—and so on.

Cecília had two outing dresses and Cema two pairs of shoes because she had already received one as a present from her godmother. Hence, my mother would use one of Cecília's dresses and a pair of Cema's shoes. For my father, we would buy a beautiful blue suit. We would also buy a striped tie and a pair of white socks. We borrowed from Zé's cousin a pair of shoes for him and we fixed up a shirt that only had some cuts on its collar. On my graduation day, everyone was nervous but they all got ready on time for the ceremony.

My dad cut Zezinho's hair, that of Dirceu and other men in the family. Afterwards, Joãzinho cut my father's hair. Due to so many involved and the fact that much preparation was involved, we ended up arriving a little late . I showed them where to sit and I went ahead to sit among my fellow graduates. From where I was, I could see my family dressed up in their church outfits. From time to time, I encouraged them with a little smile. My father was sitting by my mother. They were following my contagious gestures with their attentive eyes.

My mother was also watching through the lenses of my father, who to his delight, adjusted his collar as a gesture that all was well and that I was doing fine. I was called up to receive my certificate. They, my parents, could not limit their excitement to just clapping for me. They stood up and clapped while standing. They had opened hands, free and noisy. Likewise, my brothers and sisters also lost their timidity and clapped, pointing me out and making me feel as if I was going to receive the key to heaven.

The director waited patiently for each excitement to recede, knowing full well that their time was up and waiting for the graduates to return to their place. At the end of giving out the certificates, I was invited to make a speech since I was selected as the valedictorian.

Once again, my father stood up, adjusted the knot of his tie, and maintained a royal posture. In order to hear me, he disregarded all etiquette, and cupped his hands around his ears. All the formalities came to an end. I went to meet them so that we could return home together. Princess-like, I gave my certificate to my father, the king of the moment, who in turn, wrapped it in a handkerchief and carried it as if it were a crystal vase.

Upon arriving home, full of excitement, we continued to relive the events of the ceremony. We laughed about our clapping well beyond the allowed time; about my father making gestures with his ears and hands; about the director's attitude when he saw us behaving as if we owned the entire location. At some point, my mother interrupted all the euphoria and said:

– Now is when you will truly laugh your hearts out.
– She signaled my father with her elbow. – Show them Mariano.

Pretending to be doing magic, he took off his shoes from his feet and showed us: two big pock-marks disfigured the front and back of his feet. I was quite ecstatic. All that for me; just for me. All of that pain just to see me get my certificate. I could not contain myself.

- I am sorry, father.
- Sorry for what? I should ask for your forgiveness. Look at that! I forgot to use the socks. Imagine if one of your friends had seen me. God forbid that I embarrass you!

He thought for a while, and then, continued his conversation:

- And you know what? If need be, I will put on the shameful shoes and everything else; and return there to clap for you all over again.

Once again, a slight wave of laughter circulated within the room. Dirceu asked for his parents' blessing so as to go to bed. Others did the same thing and I was about to do the same when I saw my father looking for something.

- What are you looking for, father?
- I am wondering where I left the diploma. I am going to sleep with it under my pillow so as to have sweet dreams.

Fluctuating Energy

With a certificate in my pocket, I went out in search of a job. I found one in a school as a substitute teacher—teaching for the whole year. I was charged with teaching primary school students who were "leftovers" from teachers who, being very effective in their profession, preferred adult students who were in the process of learning to read and write.

In the school's patio, I endured many moments of discomfort in the doubtful eyes of the director and the students' parents who, incredibly, were looking at me and secretly commenting as if they had something to hide about me. All that was left, indeed, was for them to ask me if I had a certificate to prove my qualifications.

The bell rang for class to start and my little brats came in somewhat agitated and noisy. Only a light complexioned, beautiful, and tender girl hid behind the door and was crying quietly. I ran to see if I could get her to enter the classroom.

- I am afraid of a black teacher – she told me, pure and simple.

So much fear mixed with sweetness overwhelmed me. I looked for convincing arguments.

- I am going to tell you some fairy tales and ...

– What happened? – The director had come to conduct routine inspection.

I told her what had happened and she quickly found a solution.

– Not to worry. I will put in her different class.

I reacted immediately. I calmed down and pulled myself together.

– Please, leave her so we can get to understand each other better. If by closing time, she does not enter the class, you can take her to the other class.

The director accepted my proposal and left hurriedly. I then realized that it was not enough time for me to prove my equality and competence to a new group of people. But I needed such an opportunity for my own sake, and for hers. Other students took advantage of the situation with this strange student by the door as she kept analyzing, inspecting, and judging me with her suspicious, lively, and attentive eyes. I needed to give more explanation than normal and I was more impatient.

Thus tormented, I spent my whole day worried about this student. Even during my break time, I went to her, talking and talking, explaining things to her. I would be talking to her while looking at the class. It was as if I spent my whole day remembering my own childhood due to this unfortunate experience. The joy of learning and drawing. The pleasant aroma of lunch time, games, and singing; lies of innocence, since dreaming for kids is perceived as reality. During the break, while other teachers were having coffee and discussing how their classes went, I stayed at the patio. Perhaps I would have some new idea.

I saw her among other children. I approached her and asked for a piece of her food. She gave me some, somewhat undecided and startled. I decided to go further.

– I would like you to enter the class after lunch break. That way, you can sit on my chair and watch my purse while I teach.

I left without waiting for her answer. Fear. Soon, we returned to class. She sat on my chair and kept her things beside mine. I "needed" a pen. I asked her. She opened my purse like someone opening a coffin, and passed the pen to me. She smiled reluctantly. During class, I asked for anyone who could draw to raise their hands. Everyone raised their hands and she also knew how to draw. She drew a rectangular dog without a tail.

– Your dog is very funny – I told her, smiling. – He has no tail?
– It is not mine. It belongs to my grandmother. When my grandfather drinks, and is out of control, he runs to him and puts his tail within his thighs.

She lowered her head and drew a blue dog. At the end of class, she gathered her stuff gently. I noticed that she was taking slow steps and avoiding other kids. She wanted to tell me something. I was impatient. I knew that whatever it was, they must be answers to the indirect questions I had asked her. She chose the time, held my skirt and asked:

– Tomorrow, would you let me sit close to my cousin, Gisele? I will watch your purse from there as well. Tomorrow, I will bring bread and butter for lunch; do you like bread and butter?
– I love it.

- I will give you a big chunk, okay?
- Thank you. We have a deal.
- See you tomorrow.
- See you tomorrow.

The following day, there she was. First in the row; light and sweet. At first sight, she appeared to be coming towards me but the inspector of students held her hand and made her return to her place because she had already given the second signal. I looked at her and smiled. Timidly, she gestured to me that she had brought the promised lunch and did not want to call the attention of the inspector to herself. So there was, my bread and butter. It was only then that I understood everything that my father had been trying to teach me, in short, parabolic codes.

Ancestral feelings escaped from the uterus, the uterus of my roots; they have imprinted permanent laws of all my days. Since my childhood, I have carried a heavy burden, forced to treat loaded contents and wounds that have been invented for the coffin of reductionism. Prone to my messianic mission and style, I am a pastor of my people; I fulfill with pleasure the right and responsibility to take them to harmonious places. My coat of arms I have discovered and keep always ready; above, below, and in the middle: the magic of words.